MISSING LYNX

KODIAK POINT, BOOK SEVEN

EVE LANGLAIS

EveLanglais.com

Copyright © 2020/2021 Eve Langlais

Cover Art 2020 © Amanda Kelsey ~ RazzDazz Design

Produced in Canada

Published by Eve Langlais

1606 Main Street, PO Box 151, Stittsville, Ontario, Canada, K2S1A3

http://www.EveLanglais.com

E-ISBN: 978 177 384 169 4

Print ISBN: 978 177 384 170 0

PROLOGUE

*T*he rabbit appeared well fed for this time of the year. Plump. Juicy.

Mine.

Perched above, her claws digging into a tree branch, Rilee practically drooled at the thought of sinking her teeth into it. How long since her last full meal?

Too long. But then again, she wasn't one to get regular nutrition even growing up. Mom had other uses for the government subsidies. Ones that didn't involve paying to feed a cumbersome child.

Her stomach rumbled, reminding her that she couldn't keep neglecting it. It needed food.

Meaning she had to hunt.

Before her dinner could hop away, she pounced, her silent leap not alerting her prey. A cat always landed on its feet. She killed it swiftly because only psychos played with their food and only dumb animals ate it raw.

She wasn't a simple-minded beast. She'd cook the meat. It wouldn't take long to get a fire going back at camp, and with the salt and pepper she'd filched from that fast food place, she could even season it. Gourmet camping.

A better option than the nasty shelters in the city. She refused to live in a cage.

With her catch clenched in her jaws, she trotted back in the direction of her cave, a literal hole in a rocky hill she currently called home. A temporary thing until she could put some money away and get herself a real place with hot water. And a toilet. She really missed a toilet. A hole in the ground just wasn't the same.

She had no problem navigating the rocks leading up the gravelly slope to her Flintstone-ish abode. She'd hung a tarp over the entrance to keep some of the drafts and weather out. The ledge in front held the remains of her last fire, the pile of ash hopefully hiding an ember that would make her task easier.

But she couldn't do that while in her feline shape. Powerful. Fleet of foot. Beautiful. But a lynx couldn't start a fire or make dinner. Time to put her clothes back on.

As the rabbit hit the ground, she saw it: a plastic tag inside the rabbit's ear.

How could she have missed it? She nudged it with her nose and uttered a low growl of discontent. The tag uttered a faint vibration, the slight hum indicating it was transmitting. Stupid tracking device. She'd wager she knew who'd tagged it. Those annoying science folk, traipsing around in her woods, marking everything in sight. Writing papers about the migratory habits of the wildlife using modern-day GPS trackers. And she'd brought the stupid thing to her doorstep.

Technically speaking, no one was allowed to camp in these woods. And a lynx in these parts was unheard of. She couldn't be found. Only one person knew where she was and had probably already forgotten the moment she got her next fix.

Grabbing the rabbit once more in her jaws, Rilee bounded back down the slope, trotting quickly into the forest. She wanted to get it as far as she could from her camp. She'd remove the tracker and drop it in the creek where it could float away.

Bye, bye, problem.

This would actually work out better. Since she was already by the water, she'd have a quick sluice, clean her dinner, and then head back to her cave for a night of reading—because she'd brought a few books, salvaged from the garbage bin behind the library. She didn't care if half the cover was torn or a few pages stained. It beat only having her thoughts for company.

The crack of a branch froze her. Instantly, she crouched low and let the rabbit fall out of her mouth. Her ears twitched, the tufts of hair on them more than just decorative, her hearing acute.

Nothing unusual to smell, just the regular moldering of leaves, the musk of a squirrel. The cracking could have been naturally caused, but her coiled tension insisted someone watched.

With twilight falling, visibility lessened. Her gaze scanned the forest, her vision sharp despite the increasing shadows. She'd never seen anything big in these woods. Nothing that would threaten a predator like herself.

By the time she noticed the glint of goggles, it was already too late. Still, she didn't panic. She'd run into humans before, their excitement over getting a picture of a rare lynx amusing. The person stalking her didn't have a camera but a gun.

Which they fired.

She blinked at the point of impact, expecting to see blood. Instead, a cylinder with a bright tuft on the end jutted from her body.

She'd been doped! She began to run.

A man shouted, "Don't let her get away. Shoot her again."

More darts struck, and she tried to escape, but her limbs betrayed her. She folded onto the ground. Her eyes shut.

She woke in a cage.

CHAPTER 1

*T*alk about boring. Banished to small-town, middle-of-nowhere Alaska. Mateo sighed. When his boss suggested he should lie low—because apparently someone had shot a video of a tiger entering an alley and a naked man walking out—he'd hoped to spend it on a beach. Maybe take his mother to Italy for a visit, which would earn him some pasta points. No such luck.

Instead, the big boss had said, "You're going to Kodiak Point."

Which, according to the internet, only possessed a paved road to civilization a few months out of the year. Once winter hit, they relied on the dangerous ice highways.

And this was to be his home for the next little bit.

Mateo whined a little. "Send me anywhere but there. How about Afghanistan? Surely you have someone I can spy on there. Kill? Maul?" The last emerged hopeful.

Bitching didn't fly with his boss. "Are you defying a direct order? Which, I will add, came about because you were dumb. As a rock. And not an interesting rock, but the boring kind you use in ditches because it's not even good enough for the driveway."

The mouthful had Mateo blinking. "Uh." He'd been so roundly insulted there was only one comeback. "Wait until I tell my mother." It emerged as a threat. A valid one. No one wanted to deal with her.

"I'll handle your mother. It won't be so bad," his buffalo of a boss said. But don't call him Bill. Terrence could get huffy and stamp his foot when that happened.

"And what are you going to tell the hicks in charge of this town?"

"Nothing, yet. You're not going there in an official capacity."

"Little confused, boss. I thought you wanted me keeping an eye on this place."

"I do, but on the down-low. I don't want to possibly tip anyone off about our concerns. When the time is right, I'll talk to the alpha in charge. So relax. Try and enjoy yourself. I hear the fishing and hunting is excellent."

"In the winter?" he said rather doubtfully.

"Worst case, you sleep most of the day and find yourself a cushiony companion to play with while you wait for spring."

Put in those terms, it didn't sound horrible. And he did like playing in the snow.

"Who knows, maybe you'll love it and want to stay," Terrence added.

"Why would I want to stay?" The exclamation burst from him.

"Maybe you'll meet 'the one.' Pop out a few cubs. Live happily ever after."

"You forgot the yelling and the shoe throwing." He remembered what it was like at home growing up. But it was even worse when, for a few months after his father's death, the house became deathly silent except for late in the night when he'd hear his mother cry.

Never.

"Don't knock it until you've tried it," his happily married boss said.

"No way. Not happening."

I'd rather die than get hitched.

Unlike many, he didn't believe in a fated mate. As if he could look at someone and know they were *the one.* His mother claimed to have had it with his father. A widow since Mateo was nine, she'd never brought a man home for him to meet.

She clung a little tight to her only son. She also overcompensated, hence the amount of baggage that went with Mateo to Kodiak Point. He'd made sure none of the bags was large enough for her to climb in. She'd done that once on a trip to Peru.

She'd emerged from the massive trunk that was

EVE LANGLAIS

supposed to contain field supplies and smiled. "Surprise."

He'd refused to talk to her for a week after that stunt.

The ride into Kodiak Point proved sketchy, with winter just setting in. The ice roads, spanning over lakes, showed few signs of cracking and moisture. A crisp layer of snow covered most of the area except for the hard-packed ice they travelled over.

He wouldn't deny it made him nervous when they went over bodies of water. If the ice happened to fail as they crossed, he'd be in for a polar swim.

But they made it to Kodiak Point, along with their cargo. The small settlement was not quite big enough for the word town, and just as rustic as expected, with a caribou trotting down the icy road, pulling a sled with a woman and child riding inside.

He'd never embarrass himself like that.

"That's Kyle and his family. He's practicing for the Slush Races," his driver, Boris, said. The name suited his demeanor. The big burly man wore a perpetual scowl.

"Do I dare ask what that is?" he asked.

"Yearly event during the spring melt when shit turns to mud and slush."

"And what's the winner get?" he asked, leaning against the truck, which was backed into a squat building within sight of the main hamlet.

"The satisfaction of beating people." And not said but implied: Duh.

A side-by-side, also called an ATV depending on who you chatted with, whipped in their direction, a single guy behind the wheel of the utility sport vehicle.

Boris said, "That's the alpha."

Greeted by the clan leader himself, who turned out to be a large man with dark hair and a matching beard. "Reid Carver. Clan Leader of Kodiak Point." Reid held out his hand to Mateo, a very human gesture. Shifters relied on scent for greeting.

He shook it. "Nice to meet you."

Reid gestured to the ornery driver. "I see you've met my second, Boris."

"You forgot to add enforcer if your ass gets out of line," grumbled the moose, who'd probably give him a run for his money in a bare-knuckle fight.

"I'm sure Mateo knows better than to cause any problems," Reid stated.

"The first rule of shifter club is there is no shifter club. Yeah. I know." Although that rule was being bent quite a bit lately. They'd had issues since some twisted fellow down south, by the name of Parker, had exposed them. While they'd managed to more or less contain the fallout and convince humans he'd lied about shifters existing, they now had dragons to contend with.

Fucking dragons, which was kind of cool since he'd never suspected they actually existed. It also helped because it meant the human world focused on the cool creatures and not their possibly furry neighbors.

Not that dragons had meant to come out. It all

9

happened by accident because of some kind of dragon skirmish that caught the attention of the world. No amount of scrubbing could erase the many videos, but so far, people were handling it. After all, everyone loved dragons. It gave him hope that when humanity realized shapeshifters existed too, they'd accept it and not try to hunt them to extinction.

"The secret that is not so secret anymore." Reid sighed with a shake of his head. "So now, at this point, it's more about protecting us from outside backlash."

"Because a bunch of people living in relative isolation isn't suspicious at all." Mateo rolled his eyes.

"Watch your mouth, kitty cat," growled Boris.

"Or what? Does the truth bother you?"

Before the moose could bristle further, Reid stepped in. "He's right."

But Boris wasn't convinced. "I don't see what's so suspicious about a thriving community."

"Thrive too much and you'll have outsiders trying to get in," was Mateo's reply. "I've seen it before. Shifters pushed out of their towns and homes because humans rushed in thinking they'd found the next fool's gold."

"So it's bad the town is prospering?" Boris shook his head. "That's dumb."

"But easy to fix," Mateo said.

"What would you suggest?" Reid began walking back to his side-by-side, obviously expecting Mateo to follow.

"Hold on a second," Boris snapped. "Why the fuck

are you asking this stranger?"

"Because this stranger is only saying aloud something I've been worrying about. Problem is I'm not sure how to keep us viable while not drawing attention. Maybe an outsider can see the solution I can't. So?" Reid eyed Mateo.

He had to think fast. "Quickest and easiest, lose a shipment or two."

Reid grimaced. "That kind of waste just hurts me."

"Who says it has to be wasted? You could have it stolen."

"Steal our own cargo?" Boris snorted. "Then do what with it?"

"Sell it on the black market." Mateo almost rolled his eyes at the obviousness of it.

"We're not crooks," Boris huffed angrily.

"No, but you are people trying to fly under the radar. So you have a few shipments either hijacked or lost. The how doesn't matter, nor what you do with the stuff. Just make it seem like there's a bit of an economics issue."

A pensive expression appeared on Reid's face. "That's actually not a bad idea."

"Except for the fact we don't know any black-market operators," Boris pointed out.

"I do." Mateo had contacts.

"Ain't that a surprise," grumbled the moose-headed man.

"I'm interested. Once you get settled in, come talk to me," Reid said.

Things were looking up. Planning a heist would certainly pass the time, and the place wasn't completely horrible if you could ignore the fact that winter meant only a few hours of daylight each day. This time of year, night reigned. Given he thrived in the dark, he didn't mind it as much as expected.

The local amenities weren't exactly stellar. A general store and a few small establishments, many run out of people's homes, were the extent of the shopping. Yet, for its size, it still carried just about everything a guy could need, and shipping of what they didn't have could be arranged. Pretty much every day there was someone travelling into Anchorage or other towns on that icy road either with the big semi or one of the winter-equipped vehicles.

The remote nature of Kodiak Point made it ideal for hiding. The settlement was carved out of the wilderness, and it took only one trip into the woods to experience the top-notch hunting. He had to admit it was nice to get back in touch with the wild. He'd been city living for much too long.

Less fun? Dealing with his mother. His first video call had her practically trying to crawl through the screen.

"Hi, Mamma."

"Don't you 'hi' me. Breaking my heart. Moving so far. After all I did for you." His mother started her harangue, and he sighed. He'd had to endure a daily dose of it until he left.

"It's only temporary." And also not the first occasion

he'd left home. Each time, she made a fuss.

"You will be nothing but skin and bones by the time you return. People will think I'm a poor mother," she lamented as if he didn't have a suitcase full of supplies, including real Parmesan and a grater. Because that was what he needed in the boonies, freshly grated parmesan.

"There is plenty of food here, Mamma."

"Packaged pasta and canned tomatoes." She sniffed with disdain.

"I won't lie. It's not going to be even close to as good as your food, but there is fresh fish, and the caribou steaks are apparently really good."

"Hmph." She complained a bit more. Then regaled him with stories of her work. Because sewing had such excitement happening on a daily basis. Still, he was thankful she had a job because that was the only time he'd gotten away from his mother growing up.

When her babbling turned to her friends' eligible daughters, he finally managed to say goodbye and hung up.

Being a mamma's boy wasn't always easy, but it did mean the next mail run from town had a massive care package with not dozens but hundreds of different cookies, which he gave to Reid to distribute around town. The package also contained jars of his mother's Bolognese sauce. Those he didn't share.

He ate. He planned some heists. Called some people he knew to make deals. And napped. A lot.

It was perfect.

Relaxing.

Disrupted less than a week after his arrival.

The snowmobile wasn't one he'd seen before. A place this size, it didn't take long to recognize people and vehicles on sight.

The machine was old, the windshield cracked. The rider was swathed in a patched snowsuit. The helmet came off and was placed on the seat, revealing a woman he'd never seen.

Someone new. How curious. Where did she come from?

She entered the general store, and he headed in that direction, only to skulk outside, peeking through the front window. Standing with her back to Mateo, she conversed with the guy behind the counter. When she wandered off to do some shopping, he entered, his great height giving him a visual advantage over the rows of shelving. He spotted the top of her head. If he wanted a clear glimpse of her face, he'd have to get closer.

He just had to see her.

Smell her.

Touch.

He took one step. Then stopped. What was he doing?

Being weird, that's what.

He pivoted, walked a single pace, and halted again.

Surely her sudden appearance merited investigating. He whirled again. Time to stop fucking around and confront her. It would satisfy his curiosity as to whether she was old, or hideous. Not that it mattered. If she was cute, then it seemed unlikely she'd be single.

Even if she didn't have a significant other, he wasn't looking to settle down no matter how good Francesca's eggplant Parmesan was or how flaky Marisol's pie. His mother tended to rate potentials on their cooking abilities. None of which, of course, came close to his mamma's skills.

Mateo turned the corner and into the next aisle, only to realize the woman was gone. He frowned and glanced at the next row. How had she disappeared?

He nearly jumped a foot off the floor when a soft voice said, "Is there a reason why you're stalking me?"

He whirled and gaped. "Fuck me, you are quiet on your feet."

A single brow lifted. "And you're not. Nor are you very discreet when spying."

"I wasn't spying." At her pointed stare, he grinned. "Okay, maybe I was a little. What's up with your scent?" Had she been human, this would have sounded odd, but face-to-face, he had little doubt he spoke to another shifter. The familiar feline was almost masked by the stronger scent of pine. Given her silvery coloring, a cougar, perhaps? A young one.

"I'm sorry, is bathing something you're unaccustomed to?" she queried. "Perhaps I could introduce you to some soap."

His grin widened at her sassy retort. "You know what I mean. Why do you smell like car air freshener?"

"Because I like it?"

"Interesting choice. So what are you when not pretending to be a tree?" Because he thought her really cute, if tiny, compared to him at least.

"What I am is none of your business. I don't owe you an explanation."

While he couldn't understand why she'd keep it a secret, he let it go. "I've never seen you around before."

"Because I don't live in town."

"Where do you live?" he asked. A study of the surrounding maps hadn't shown any other settlements nearby.

"You don't need to know. And I don't appreciate being interrogated by strangers." Her lips pinched.

"Name is Mateo Ricci." He held out his hand.

She eyed it but didn't shake. "You're new," she stated.

"Yup. I arrived about a week ago."

"Did no one explain that some of us come here for privacy?"

"I won't tell any of your secrets. We're all friends here." Because the second rule of shifter club was everyone supported shifter club.

"I don't need friends."

"I do. Don't suppose you'd like to go for a beer? Maybe throw some darts?"

"No."

"Do you prefer wine? I could cook you a feast. Just don't tell my mother."

Her lips flattened, and then as if she couldn't help herself, "Why can't your mother know you cook?"

"Because then she'll cry and claim I don't need her anymore, and then I'll have to eat twice as much for the next month to prove I do, and the last time I did that, I gained twenty pounds." He couldn't help a rueful peek at his gut. He struggled at times with his weight. Amur tigers were prone to storing fat.

"You're a mama's boy?" she said, almost incredulously.

"Yup. And proud of it. You close to your mother?"

"No. She's dead. And before you ask, so is my dad. My grandparents. Everyone."

"You're an orphan? That sucks."

"Wow, this is..." She shook her head. "I've got to go. Goodbye."

"Already? But you haven't even told me your name."

"Because it's not important." She turned and walked away.

He found himself blurting out, "Can I see you again?"

She paused in her departure to glance at him over her shoulder. Then stated very clearly, "No."

Then she left.

And Mateo laughed and laughed until he almost cried.

The confused boy behind the counter just had to ask, "What's so funny?"

More like ironic. Fate bitch-slapping him for what he'd said to Terrence just a week before.

"That little lady is gonna be my wife."

This tiger had found his mate.

CHAPTER 2

*R*ilee couldn't have said why she talked to the man, especially when her first impulse upon first scenting and then spotting Mateo was to run. Hide.

His presence disquieted. Especially since her feline wanted to get closer. Sniff him. Maybe give him a lick.

Had he rolled in catnip?

Not that Mateo needed help being attractive. While he might loom over her by more than a foot, and wider by even more, he had a handsome face. His Mediterranean-toned skin was offset by his jet-black hair. Even his name was sexy, and she wanted to roll it off her tongue.

Maybe he wore salmon cologne. He certainly got close enough for her to scent him. Crave him.

The brazen jerk didn't even try to hide the fact he was spying on her. It took everything she had to be brave when he confronted her. She hoped he didn't notice her racing heart.

Who was this man? What did he want? She'd not escaped only to be caught again. She thought for sure this time she'd managed to break free.

I'll never go back to a cage.

The fear had her heading for Reid Carver's office. As alpha of this town, he could reassure her. He was one of the few people who could calm her anxiety and handle the issue with the newcomer. Reid would tell him to leave her alone. And if that wasn't enough, she could always tell Boris.

And why can't I just handle this myself? Since when do I ask for help?

Entering Reid's outer office—which appeared as the building of a shipping company, the one handling the goods coming in and out of town—she encountered Tammy, Reid's wife, sitting behind the desk. A swaddled baby fed at her breast while a little boy played with large building blocks in a corner blocked off with white plastic fencing. A gentler method than her mother had used. The leash got easily tangled. She'd almost choked to death a few times. Her mother blamed her each time. *Dumb cunt. Trying to get me in trouble.*

Yeah, she wanted to die to get back at her mother. Who was the dumb one?

Tammy glanced away from the computer to smile at her. "Hey, Rilee. How was your trading haul this week?"

For a while now, Rilee had been bringing in fur and other items of interest for swapping. It meant she didn't need money and didn't leave a paper trail.

"It's been a good year for hunting," she admitted. Not that it mattered if she could bring in enough. In Kodiak Point, no one went without. "Is Reid in? I need to ask him something."

"He's actually out with the boys today. You got a problem?" Tammy asked, flipping the baby to her shoulder and burping her.

Rilee scrunched her nose, hating to ask for help, but if there was anyone she'd come to trust, it was Reid and his wife. "There's a new guy in town. Asking me lots of questions."

"You met Mateo, I see," Tammy said with a laugh. "As you noticed, he's not the shy type."

"Ya think?" she muttered.

"Don't worry about him. He's a good sort."

"Why is he here?"

"Just needed getting away from the world for a bit."

"Is he in trouble?"

"Not really. The video of him that's circulating was grainy enough it could be someone else. Still, as a precaution, *they*"—as in those who ran things behind the scenes of every town— "wanted him out of sight, out of mind."

"Someone should remind him that the people who come here often expect some privacy."

Rather than agree, Tammy frowned. "I worry about

you, Rilee." Not the first time the slightly older woman had said that.

"I'm fine."

"You say that, and yet I can't help but be concerned about you living by yourself in the woods."

"I like being alone." Liked the freedom and the quiet.

"What if something happens to you, though? What if you need help?"

Given the same question had crossed her mind, she didn't scoff, just rolled her shoulders. "I've got that walkie-talkie Reid gave me. And you know Boris and some of the others swing by to check on me a few times a week."

Tammy sighed. "And you find even that level of care too much."

For some reason, Rilee grinned. "It's nice, but also annoying. They're like hens clucking over me. Do you have enough wood? Food? How's your roof?" She rolled her eyes, even as she wouldn't admit it wasn't a bad thing after what happened to her.

Years ago, when Reid found her in the wilds, she wasn't much better than a wild animal, almost rabid in her fear. He took the time to bring her back to civilization by promising no one would ever get close enough to hurt her again.

A promise he could keep when she lived in Kodiak Point. But once she'd moved out on her own, choosing to take over a recently abandoned cabin in the woods, she knew the risk she took.

"Weather gal says there's a storm brewing to hit in a few days. A big one."

"Good thing I'll have my supplies before then," Rilee quipped before leaving Reid's office, having managed to not once cast a longing gaze at the children.

Used to be a time when she'd wanted a few ankle biters of her own. Then she spent time in a cage courtesy of a psycho and a mother who valued drugs more than her daughter. This wasn't a world that deserved children. Not to mention, she'd need a man to at least donate sperm. And who could she choose? All the good ones in town were taken.

No man. No babies. So what did her traitorous mind do? Reminded her of those hazel eyes, that playboy grin, and the dimple. Mateo had a freaking dimple.

It was almost too much. A good thing she didn't plan to see him again. With a storm about to hit, she'd be hunkered down inside her cozy place and getting important stuff done, like hand stitching some moccasins. She'd finally gotten all the tools to try.

Welcome to her exciting life.

The ATV, old and noisy but reliable, chugged as she took the path home. A good twenty-minute route that took an extra hour as she veered to check on her traps. Couldn't trade if she didn't catch anything. Fur and meat, berries in late summer. A shifter town the size of Kodiak Point, full of predators, went through a lot of food, more than they could easily have shipped in.

As for fur, despite what those tree-huggers liked to

claim, some animals reproduced rapidly unless kept under control by natural predators. Like her. The general rule of hunting was don't waste. Eat the meat, use the fur, and pluck those feathers.

Only one of her snares caught something. A grouse that went into a pot after she cleaned it. First, she'd bake it. Her mouth salivated at the thought of the crisp skin. The meat would be juicy. Once stripped of most of the meat, she tossed the bones into a pot with some water, herbs, and root vegetables to make a rich stew.

In other words, the same thing she made a few days ago, and the week before that. Good hearty food, but it was never changing. Boring.

Like her life.

However, the alternative meant dealing with people.

No thanks.

She went to sleep that night and dreamed of a certain brash man. He flirted outrageously in her dream. Tried to kiss her, which startled her awake, aware of the ache between her legs.

Only recently had that desire returned, and because she'd started reading romance again, she knew how to take care of it. Her fingers rubbed, knowing where and how to touch, heightening her arousal, but it wasn't until she closed her eyes and pictured Mateo that she came.

Annoying man. Ruining even her personal fun. She grumbled as she rolled out of bed. She'd only just met the guy and barely tolerated him. Why could she not stop thinking of him?

If an annoying twat like him could attract her, then maybe it was a sign she was well enough to think about dating.

Dating who?

She knew everyone in town. Not one ever starred in her fantasies. Perhaps a brisk walk. Some exercise would clear her mind.

She set out on foot, her snowshoes balancing her weight on the crusty snow. The branches of the forest creaked, something dumping a puff of snow. It was peaceful out here, unbroken by the sound of people. Unmarred by so-called progression.

The sun shone bright, and the air was brisk. It helped to calm her nerves. In these woods, she was safe. She didn't have to see Mateo. Didn't have to see anyone.

Except for the delivery person. They were slated to arrive early afternoon, with enough time to leave before darkness fell.

She should check her traps now in case she could send something back for credit on her next visit.

About a hundred yards from her place, she heard the snap and then the creak as one of the snares reacted. Given the bellowing that followed, it didn't take seeing to know she'd caught something big with a vocabulary that flipped from English to Italian.

What is he doing in my woods?

CHAPTER 3

"*F*uck. Fuck. Fuck." Mateo could have cursed his stupidity at walking right into the trap. Literally. It tightened around his ankles and yanked him off his feet.

In his defense, he'd not expected any snares. He'd been too busy checking out the tiny cabin he could see through the trees. Smoke poured from the chimney. Given the directions he'd been given, he knew it had to be *her* place. But whose trap?

Was she in danger? Or did someone set them as a protection for her since she lived out here alone? At least, according to those he questioned, which included the alpha, who'd growlingly warned, "Don't fuck with her."

Reverse psychology? Totally worked on his dumb ass.

Because he wanted nothing more than to see her

again. Wearing less clothes. Doing the exact thing Reid said not to do.

He blamed a restless night on the fact he'd walked unheedingly and sprung a clever snare. Then to compound his embarrassment, he might have bellowed a litany of curses, which was when he heard her yell, "Calm down. I'm coming." In but seconds, she stalked into the small clearing, wearing a plaid lumberjacket and moccasin-style boots, a rifle slung over her shoulder. She glared up at him.

"You," she growled.

"Morning, *bella.*"

"That is not my name."

He knew that. But not much else since everyone said the same thing, *Leave her alone.* "Since you won't tell me your name. I had to improvise. I chose bella for your beauty."

The complimentary nickname only served to deepen her scowl. "What are you doing here?"

"Dropping off supplies." Which was just an excuse to see her. His mate. He'd not been able to get her out of his mind. Frightening in some respects, and yet, he'd heard about the mating urge enough to understand what was happening to him. Humans had love at first sight. Animals relied on instinct and pheromones. He'd not believed in it until the urge slammed into him, demanding he touch her. Mark her. Maybe pee on a few trees in the area to show she belonged to him.

A good thing he'd held off on the urine bit, as she didn't appear happy to see him. Yet. His mamma always told him he could charm an angel out of Heaven if he wanted.

"I don't see any supplies," she pointed out.

"They're with the snowmobile."

"Don't see a machine." She gave an exaggerated look around.

"Because it's over there." He pointed to the woods to the west.

"So you parked it and walked? Why? Trying to sneak up on me? Because I should warn you that's a good way to get shot."

"I thought I smelled something."

"Over the sled's fumes?"

Drat, she had a reply for every excuse. "I have a good nose."

"Not that great apparently or you wouldn't have gotten caught. First time I ever snared myself a tiger. Wonder how much I could get for you in town?" She smirked.

"You laid this trap?"

"Is this where you show your chauvinistic side and tell me it's not bad for a woman?"

He grinned. "Actually, I was going to say my mother would approve."

The reply had her chewing her lower lip. "Your mother hunts?"

"Not exactly, but she does cook and believes in only using fresh ingredients."

She cocked her head. "Do you talk about your mother a lot?"

He could have lied, but a mamma's boy would always get caught. Best get it out in the open now. "I love my mother. Smartest and strongest woman I know."

"Apparently not the greatest mother since she neglected to teach you that when a woman says no, I don't want to see you, you should respect that."

"I didn't come to see you, though, but to help out the community. Your regular delivery guy had to fly out and deal with some family problem." Mainly Mateo giving him tickets to see a hockey game in Vancouver. "I was asked if I could give a hand." More like he volunteered quite vociferously until Reid sighed and said, *Fine but don't come crying to me if she blows off your balls.*

"And you of course jumped at the chance to be a good resident."

She saw right through him.

So he changed tactics. "Fine. I wanted to see you again. Can you blame me with your sunny disposition?" Yeah, he yanked her tail, and enjoyed it, especially as her expression turned sucked-on-a-lemon taut.

"Anyone ever tell you that you're annoying? Especially given you're so cheerful about it."

"All the time. My mother usually says it's a good thing I was a cute cub growing up or she would have sold me for money."

Her face turned to stone before she turned and strode away.

"What did I say?"

She didn't reply.

"Where are you going? Still hanging upside down in a tree over here!" he reminded.

"I know."

"Shouldn't you do something about it?"

She paused on the edge of the clearing and glanced at him over her shoulder. "I'll release you when I'm done unloading my supplies." With those words, she left. Like actually took off and a moment later he heard the chug of a motor.

Fuck him, but she really wanted nothing to do with people. Reid had warned him. As had Boris, whose exact words were, "Girl is broken. If you upset her, I'll break you even worse." But the one who truly scared him was Boris's pregnant wife, Jan, who put a gun to the back of his head and whispered, "Keep in mind, while my husband will hurt you, I'll kill you. Double tap. You'll never rise again."

Rather than be afraid, he laughed. How could he not? He'd found his kind of people. Their words told him more than the fact they had a propensity for violence; it spoke of their deep bond with everyone in this town, even for a standoffish woman who'd been hurt.

By whom? Given her reaction to the last thing he'd said—a joke about a mother selling her child—he cringed to imagine. Who could ever harm a kid?

How could he show her that some people were worthy of trust?

He should start by proving he had some brains.

What must she think, him getting caught by a snare then unable to release himself? Pathetic. How could he prove he'd make her a fine mate if she thought he needed to be taken care of?

His stomach muscles protested as he pulled himself up enough that he could saw at the rope holding his ankles. He dropped the knife into the snow before he fell, managing to twist and land on his feet. Not that there was anyone there to admire his agility. She really had left.

He had no problem following, especially since he heard his snowmobile revving in the distance. Given the coordinates he'd entered into his phone, they weren't far from her place. He jogged down the trail and arrived in time to see her unstrapping the load in the sledge that acted as a trailer.

She slewed a gaze his way but said nothing as she hauled a case of canned preserves into the log cabin. Not a big place, especially compared to the homes in town. It was made of actual logs, notched together at the corners. A window to the left of the door. Not a big one. The chimney from the steeply pitched roof puffed smoke. To the side of the cabin and wrapping around the corner right to the front door was an untouched woodpile. A peek around the side showed a trail going to the back. When the weather was good, she made the extra effort to get the stuff farthest away.

Smart.

Unlike him. He entered the cabin, carrying two large bins at a time, which, in retrospect, was dumb.

Yes, it showcased his fine muscles, but it also meant they would empty the sledge much too fast.

Despite the pitched roof, the ceiling was low inside, planks of wood draped across notched beams. She saw him staring and said, "They're lined with insulation on the other side but loose so I can remove them in the summer."

"To let the hot air rise," he muttered. Then frowned. "Does it get that hot?"

"Maybe not the kind you're used to down south but enough that you're hot and sweaty when trying to sleep."

The thought of her glistening and wet...

His desire hovered as he stared at her. Her lips parted. Did she feel it, the connection between them—

That broke as she walked out the door to grab another load. He followed, and realized they were almost done. Apparently, a person living alone didn't need much stuff.

The moment he dropped the two large jugs of water, she was ready for him to leave.

"Thanks. Bye."

"I don't suppose I could trouble you for a drink. I'm awfully thirsty." He gave her his most engaging smile. The one that made his mother roll her eyes and then feed him. Often. A growing Amur tiger needed a lot of nourishing.

"I only have water."

"I like water." Usually as an ice cube in a chilled glass of something alcoholic.

She stomped to a sink, which was fed from a jug on the counter. She poured him a cup and offered it, careful to not touch him.

He took a sip. "Have you lived here long?"

It was hard to tell. The cabin appeared as if it had sat here quite some time, but inside, it lacked the homey accents that would make it a home. No pictures or knickknacks, just practical stuff. A single bed with bins tucked underneath. A table with a single straight-back chair. Shelves ran the perimeter of the room, about a foot below the roofline, and held books. Lots of books.

There was a single plush seat, the kind that could rock, in front of a woodstove, with more books stacked beside it. The counter that ran the length of one wall was stacked underneath with food. The shelves over it held dishes and spices. A simmering pot cooked on her woodstove, emitting a savory scent. As per the sparse intel he'd managed to acquire from town, she lived alone.

"I've been here a little while."

"I'm surprised you don't have a pet." While some might think it ironic a shifter would have a furry critter underfoot, for many, it provided a simple companion that sometimes understood them better than humans ever could.

"Have you seen the size of this place?" She arched a brow. "Besides, I like being alone."

"You do?" He glanced around. Tried to imagine what it would be like to have no one else around. Nor even a television or radio. No sound at all. "That seems very…lonely."

"Don't start. Did Tammy put you up to this?"

"What?" The question confused him.

"She asked you to deliver the groceries, didn't she?"

"Actually, it was Reid." He skipped the part where he begged.

She frowned. "Reid and not Tammy?"

"Would you feel better if I said Boris threatened to cut off my balls if I upset you."

Her lips twitched. "Yes."

"And Jan said she'd make sure she blew my brains so wide I'd never come back to life as a zombie."

She cracked a small smile. "Sounds like Jan."

"You have a lot of folks in town who care for you."

She shrugged. "They're good people."

"If they're so good, why do you hide in the woods?"

Rather than reply, she asked him point-blank, "Why are you so interested in me?"

His mother didn't raise a liar. "You're my mate."

She blinked, and her face went through a myriad of flashing expressions. "No."

Just the one word, but scent didn't lie. She wasn't hiding behind a cardboard green tree freshener this time.

He grinned. "Yeah, you are."

She shook her head. "No. I'm not. So you can get that stupid idea out of your head."

"How can you be sure? Maybe you need to smell me a little closer?"

"I can smell you just fine. Still not interested."

He reached for her, just a light brush of his fingers over her hand, and she jumped as if he'd tasered her—which he'd seen before. Yet, in her case, rather than jiggling with electrical current, her eyes widened.

In fear.

Of him.

Unacceptable.

Which was why he immediately raised his hands and backed away.

That didn't stop her from grabbing the shotgun by the door and aiming it in his direction. "Get out."

"Now, bella."

"I said out."

Given he'd gravely erred, he knew better than to argue. Besides, he didn't trust himself to speak.

Too many things came clear in that instant. The main point being someone had scared his future mate.

Not just scared but obviously hurt her.

And that just wasn't something he could tolerate.

Tell me who I have to kill.

CHAPTER 4

*R*ilee was still shaking. Mateo hadn't done a single threatening thing, just a brief touch of skin. To say it had startled was an understatement.

Excitement. A shot of heated lust.

Then fear. Panic.

At least he'd not argued and had left before she had to shoot him. Once he was gone, she barred the door and leaned on it long after the chugging motor of the sled faded.

Hated that she'd so quickly fallen into that trap. Would she regress to that ugly time after Reid had rescued her when a harmless touch had kept her hiding in her room the rest of that week?

When she'd first arrived in Kodiak Point—waking in an actual bedroom with its own three-piece bath instead of a cage—she was little better than a wild animal, barely remembering how to be human. She'd refused to switch out of her lynx, snarling and snapping at Reid every time he came into her room. He never harmed her. He would just stand for a second and say, "You're safe here. I will protect you."

As if she'd believe him.

The food he brought—along with utensils— surely was a ploy. But she still ate it.

Belly full, she eyed the shower. It had been...too long since she'd had one. Or seen a bar of soap.

Not that she dared use them. She couldn't let anyone see what she was. Bad things would happen.

As the first two days out of her captivity passed, she waited for Reid to abuse her. Make demands. Threats.

He didn't do a thing. Just kept bringing her food. She refused to talk, staying in her lynx form, which proved challenging when it was time to go to the bathroom. Gripping that toilet wasn't the highlight of her day. Yet, it was the start of finding her humanity again. Her will to live. To be...herself.

That wakening awareness was when she realized she might be able to trust Reid. Not only had he not harmed her, she wasn't a prisoner. The door to her room wasn't locked.

Exiting into a hallway as mundane as her room, with its scuffed wood floors and neutrally painted plaster walls, she'd sniffed. She still remembered being overwhelmed by scents, Reid's being the strongest. But there were others too. With that special tang that meant they were different, like her.

She slipped silently down a staircase and prowled into the living room, a slinking shadow that clung to the walls while a woman played with a small child. A baby who lay on its back, kicking feet and hands. Gurgling.

The sight stopped her in her tracks. Reid had brought her to his home. Trusted her around his mate and child.

Bit by bit, she returned to herself, but she was unable to stem her nightmares.

Reid tried, but ultimately, he didn't understand. Only Boris comprehended the difficulties with PTSD.

There was a time Rilee doubted she'd ever get over what happened. After her time in the cage, she couldn't tolerate hardly anyone around her at first. Reid, with his calming presence and commanding voice, helped her stave off more than one panic attack. Boris became acceptable, mostly because she saw how the man catered to his tiny wife, Jan, and he treated Rilee like a daughter. The kind of gruff father who didn't hug or say, "I love you," but offered to kill people on a regular basis if they might have offended her. It was one of the nicest things anyone ever said to her.

They helped her heal from her ordeal. Boris especially knew how to sit quietly in a corner of her room when she woke screaming from her nightmares. Never said anything. He didn't need to because he understood what happened inside her head. How the past refused to stay buried.

But eventually it didn't consume her every waking moment. She learned to leave the house. To even tolerate other people. What she couldn't stand were small spaces or being touched. When she first decided to move out, she'd worried her cabin might remind her too much of the cage she'd lived in for too long. For the first few days, she'd kept the door open whenever she was inside.

More than three years later, she could keep it closed, and even shutter her windows if the drafts got too bad.

However, she still didn't like being touched. And Mateo obviously got that point because he'd stalked out of her home. He'd been angry, but not because she rejected him. No. If she read him correctly, he was mad because she'd been scared of him.

Now that he knew she would never look at him like he wanted her to, he wouldn't return.

Probably for the best.

So why did it make her so sad?

CHAPTER 5

The moose man tried to stand in Mateo's way, but he wasn't about to be stopped. He lifted Boris and set him aside, which caused Jan, Boris's wife and the receptionist of the day, to let out silvery peals of laughter.

When the moose huffed through his nose, Mateo shook his finger. "Later we will play. Right now, I need to speak to the alpha. About Rilee."

"What about Rilee? What did you do?" Boris bristled, his fists clenching.

"I didn't do shit. But someone obviously did," he snarled.

Jan sounded surprised as she said, "She told you?"

"No!" he barked. "But you just confirmed my suspicions. I want to know who. And most importantly, are they dead?"

Boris couldn't have frowned harder if he tried. "It's not that simple."

"Meaning they aren't." He glowered. "I want a name."

"I can't—"

He grabbed hold of the big man and had him on the floor in a second. Boris didn't fight back, which was kind of disappointing.

Then again, he didn't have to. Jan and her gun stood behind him. "Let Boris go."

"You wouldn't shoot me."

"Hurt my hubby and you'll find out," she said much too sweetly.

"Does your wife always fight your battles?" Mateo asked.

"All the time." Boris snorted. "I've given up on explaining that it's emasculating when she tries to protect me."

"Oh, be quiet. You know you love it. Now, if we're done discussing my awesomeness, get off my husband."

"Fine," Mateo huffed.

"What the fuck is going on?" growled Reid, the door to his office suddenly open.

"Pretty boy is all bent out of shape on account he figured out Rilee had some trouble in her past," Boris declared.

"She told you?" Reid asked with a surprised arch of brow. He also juggled a child in his arms.

"No, she didn't, but it's pretty fucking obvious someone hurt her."

"Yeah. Someone did. And badly," Reid said in a low, grave tone.

"Tell me about it."

When Reid hesitated, Jan intervened. "It's not like it's a secret." She glanced at Mateo. "When she got here, she was messed up. Given she was prone to running, we had to tell people about her. Especially since no one could touch her in the beginning." Her lips pressed into a tight line. "I swear, if we ever find the bastard who hurt her, I'll put a bullet in his head myself."

"Get in line," Reid muttered. "And I guess there's no harm in giving you warning about Rilee."

Jan held out her arms. "Give me the boy. He shouldn't hear this kind of thing."

Jan took the child, and Reid led Mateo into his office. "Have a seat."

Mateo did, mostly so he wouldn't pace. He got the feeling he wouldn't like the story.

It took Reid a moment to start. "I found Rilee about five years ago."

"Found? Was she lost?"

"Yes. In more ways than one. It started when I got a report about a wild cat terrorizing campers, destroying campsites. Before they could send someone out to shoot it, I paid a visit."

"You knew it was a shifter?" Mateo asked.

Reid shook his head. "No, but there was something deliberate in the attacks that made me wonder. I went to the national park where the trouble was and tracked down the cat causing the ruckus."

Given Reid was a Kodiak bear, it wasn't hard to

imagine even another predator backing down. "You calmed her down and brought her here."

Reid snorted. "If only it were that easy. I almost lost an eye our first meeting. It took me two weeks of bribing Rilee with food and talking out loud to no reply before she finally met me face to face without taking a swipe. The only reason I managed to get her out of that park was because the conservation authority caught up to her and shot her. Which, I will add, didn't make her more amenable to my aid, but given she passed out, I was able to do what needed to be done."

"Which explains how she ended up here, but not how she ended up in those woods out of her mind in the first place."

Reid scrubbed his face. "This is the part that's ugly. She's only told me tiny bits of her story. The basic outline being she got captured while in her cat shape."

"A lynx, which is rare and probably a coup for any zoo, private or not."

"Private. When she woke up, she found herself in a cage, the resident of a menagerie owned by a poacher."

"Fucking assholes." All shifters were aware of and hated them. It was why most of them eschewed firearms, because of the casual nature of the killing. However, changing times meant they'd had to change too. In a battle, rushing headlong at a guy aiming a gun was dumb.

"It gets worse than just being a slave in a cage. The

man who caught her was a sadist. And he knew what she was. He tried to force her to shift."

"Force... She was tortured?" The revelation was a sucker-punch.

"Yes, but I never had her relive the details. I couldn't, not when she still suffers nightmares from the experience. When she stayed with me, she used to wake in utter terror a few times a night."

His heart clenched. "She escaped, obviously."

"She did. Eventually." Said softly and dread filled Mateo's stomach.

"How long was she his prisoner?"

"Five years. She was captured just after her eighteenth birthday."

"Five..." The length of time boggled the mind. It also explained even more about her. Having spent a few months incarcerated in prisons here and there because of some of his activities, he could sympathize. It was then he clued in though. "Wait, if she refused to shift, then she spent those five years as her cat."

Reed nodded. "It's a wonder she retained any of her humanity."

It also explained why she didn't feel comfortable in a town surrounded by people, but at the same time, she shouldn't let her past condemn her to a life alone. Problem being, how to get close to her?

When he got his next care package from his mamma, he had an idea. With a pack strapped to his back, he set off on foot to pay her a visit, this time watching for traps.

Only to have her sneak up on him again!

CHAPTER 6

*R*ilee cocked her gun, knowing the sound would alert him. "What are you doing?"

"I brought you a present."

"On foot?"

But not sneaking. He sauntered down the path, without a care in the world. "The snow machines are noisy. I like listening to nature." A reply she could find no argument with.

"You wasted your time. I don't want a present."

"Not just any present. My mother's secret sauce.

"Which I don't need."

He guffawed. "Says someone who's obviously never tasted it. Trust me when I say you've never had better Bolognese."

"Maybe I don't like red sauce on my stuff."

"Probably because you never tried Mamma's," he boasted.

"Are you seriously here to harass me about eating your mom's dumb sauce?"

"Harass? Never. Although I am offended you called the sauce dumb. It is the ambrosia that with one bite will empty everything in your head."

"So eating it will make me dumb?" She eyed him and smirked. "Explains a lot." A gun in hand made her bold. That and living in Kodiak Point for years. Brave enough to even pull a tiger's tail.

Many a guy would have freaked that she'd insulted him. Mateo? The dimple deepened as he laughed. "You mock, and you are skeptical, but I shall prove my words by making you dinner."

Let him come inside, where he would once more consume all the space and render her hyper aware of him? "No." She moved away from him, having already said too much. She wasn't one to have conversations or string more than a few sentences together at a time.

Although, of late, her visits in town had involved more people. She'd even spent the night at Reid's place a few times recently, offering to babysit so they could go out. She'd spent an evening binge-watching shows on streaming services.

Could it be she was finally ready to live among people again?

Mateo kept pace, not at all deterred. "Don't be so hasty. What if I told you I brought flour and eggs so I can make the pasta from scratch?"

She eyed him, his massive size, that dimple in his

cheek, and tried to imagine him elbow deep in dough. "You can make pasta?"

"Since I was knee high, and I can show you how."

"Why would I bother when it's easier to dump some packaged stuff into a pot of boiling water?"

He actually shuddered. "Don't let my mother hear you say that. She's been known to go on for hours about a certain orange pasta on the market that's super popular with folks."

"I love that stuff!" she exclaimed.

He groaned. "Oh, bella, please, you have to let me show you what real pasta tastes like."

There was something about him that made her light inside and brought a smile to her lips. And therein lay the danger. What if she forgot for a moment and let him get close?

Would he betray her?

Even if he didn't, what if he flirted with her and she freaked out? Next time he touched her, what if she did shoot?

Or started screaming?

She couldn't have said which was worse. Best to ensure it never happened.

"What part of I like to be alone did you not grasp?"

"How can you be sure you prefer it if you've never tried my company?" He didn't give up.

"This is harassment."

"This is me asking you to give me a chance because I've got a gut feeling we're meant for each other."

A sharp pang, a desire for it to be true, hit her. Then

reality rushed in. "What makes you think you're so special?"

"I'm glad you asked. I am very good looking."

"Passable," she said, lying through her teeth.

"Have a most excellent personality."

"According to who?"

"My mother. She also says I have the sweetest, roundest, yummy cheeks."

Before she could stop herself, she found herself saying. "Your cheeks are not even close to chubby. Maybe you need to eat more."

He choked. "I eat more than enough, I assure you. And don't let my mother ever hear you say I look hungry. She feeds me too much as it is. See." He lifted his shirt to show her a belly that, while not defined, looked strong and flat.

"You are not fat."

"Poke me and see."

She arched a brow. "I am not touching you."

"I forgot about that rule."

"It's not a rule but a preference."

"Which I will respect. My mother raised me right. Shifter's honor." He saluted with two fingers.

She snorted. "With how many times you've mentioned your mother, I'm surprised you ever left home."

"It was a battle with much tears. Have you ever seen a grown man cry, bella? Not pretty. But in the end, despite her swearing my leaving would probably kill her, I moved into the loft over the garage."

She stared at him. "Please tell me you're kidding. You still live at home?"

"Over the garage," he clarified. "My loft is rated as a fully functional apartment. I even pay rent and utilities."

"It's ten feet from your mother."

"More like twenty-five." And he didn't seem embarrassed by it at all.

"You know, at your age, you might want to think about getting some space. Cutting loose those apron strings."

"Why?"

"Because you're a grown man and it's weird."

"She's my mother. She needs me."

"And how does your girlfriend feel about it?" Too late she realized it looked as if she was fishing for information.

His smile couldn't have gotten any smugger. "Single. So you don't need to worry. Especially since I am not the type to double dip. If you're with me, you won't have to share me with anyone else."

"Except your mother."

"Exactly. Glad you understand. Since my father died, I'm the only family she's got left. Don't take it personally when you meet if she hates you on sight."

She knew she shouldn't ask but did it anyway. "Why would we ever meet?"

"I'd say that seems obvious, given you and I are fated to be." With those bold words, he strode off in the direction of her cabin, leaving her to gape.

This was the second time he'd made the assertion. The first time, the very idea had made her heart flutter, and then her blood chilled. A mate meant letting someone get close.

Never.

Ever.

She would set him straight. Warn him he wasted his time. She knew better than to get involved with anyone.

Entering the cabin, she immediately noticed he'd already begun to unpack his knapsack. A mason jar with red sauce inside. A canister of flour. Eggs, which he'd wrapped in a soft, light gray scarf. When the eggs were safe, he handed the scarf to her.

"This is for you."

"Why?" She scrunched the soft fabric.

"Do I need a reason to offer a gift?"

"I don't want a gift." Because those came with strings. She shoved it back at him.

"What if I said to think of it as payment?"

"For what?"

"Not killing me."

"Yet," she specified. "I haven't killed you yet."

The threat had him throwing back his head and uttering a boisterous chuckle. It was kind of contagious. She bit her lips lest she join him.

"If you're going to kill me, wait until after dinner. Because I am about to blow your taste buds," he practically purred. But it was the playful wink that made something clench between her legs.

He turned away, and a good thing too. She found herself startled and alarmed because, for the first time in a long time—a very, very long time—she felt desire for another person.

It surprised her mostly because she'd assumed that part of her life over. Sure, she masturbated, she was, after all, a healthy woman, but she never expected she'd ever want someone to be the one touching her again.

She stared at him, hearing the deep rumble of his voice as he laid out his ingredients. She waited for the fear to become unbearable. The panic as she realized they were alone in a closed room.

But much like Reid and Boris and the other people she trusted, she could relax around him. Maybe even be normal.

He certainly didn't appear to think anything was amiss with her. He grabbed things from her shelves as if he had every right, regaling her with stories of his childhood as he measured out flour and water then added eggs, kneading the whole mess, still talking. He never shut up.

She couldn't have repeated what he spoke of, other than he was amusing, often outrageous. He had a tendency of turning and just plain smiling at her, as if the sight of her made him happy.

Which was odd because she'd thought him to be a serious and grim man. That first time when he'd stalked her in the store, he'd had a dangerous look. In the forest, he kept careful watch.

But in here, with her, he showed a gentle side that

kept up a single-sided conversation and didn't appear to mind she kept a wary eye on him, waiting for the moment he'd... He'd what?

Logically she knew he wouldn't attack her. No, his plan was much worse. He offered friendship and the kind of flirting that usually happened between a man and a woman. The teasing that would have led to something more with a person a lot less broken.

She could have sent him packing anytime, but she didn't. Instead, she allowed herself to pretend for a few hours that she could be that girl who had a dinner date with a guy. The kind of girl who deserved the candles he scrounged from a shelf and sat in the middle of her small table.

The food certainly rivaled the best she'd ever eaten.

She groaned aloud at the first bite. Then blushed.

"How is it?" he asked, his voice oddly rough.

She held up a finger as she brought another forkful to her mouth. Surely, she was wrong. It couldn't have been that good.

Moan.

Even better.

"Lord fucking help me," she heard him mutter.

She glanced over to see him intent on his plate of food, sopping some of the bread she'd made yesterday, but he'd transformed. He'd slathered it with some ghee, sprinkled garlic powder on it, and then toasted it.

She joined him in enjoying the feast, doing better about holding in her sounds of enjoyment but unable to stop herself from wiping the plate clean.

When she was done shoving food into her mouth, she leaned back with a sigh and admitted, "That was really freaking good."

"I could tell," was his rumble. "I've never been more jealous of food."

"Jealous?" she said with a nervous laugh but also a flutter at the ardent look in his eyes.

"So—" Whatever he planned to say got drowned out by Ozzy's, "Mama, I'm Coming Home." He frowned. "She's early."

"Who is?"

"Mamma."

She thought he was joking. "Wait, your mother is calling? How? I don't get a cell signal."

"Satellite phone. I am not allowed to leave home without it. And. yes, it's my mother. We talk every night. Give me a second. If I don't answer, she'll freak." He rose and brought the phone to his ear, answering with a rushed, "Can I call you back, Mamma? I'm kind of busy."

Rilee's hearing was good enough to hear what was being said, but politeness had her making noise as she cleared the table.

His expression, when she glanced over, was one of forbearance. "Of course, you're important. You're my mother, who taught me everything I know, including my manners. I'm being rude to my friend."

She stiffened. Friend? She wouldn't have called them that, but then again, it had been a pleasant afternoon and early evening.

"A female friend if you must know." A pause. "No, she's not my girlfriend." He glanced at her as he said it, winked and mouthed, *Yet.*

She blushed and hoped she turned quick enough he didn't see.

He kept talking. "I haven't told you about her because we just met. If you must know, her name is Rilee." A reply a la Charlie Brown before he held the phone away from his ear and said, "Mamma says hi."

It didn't sound that way, but Rilee managed a weak, "Um, hello right back?"

He went back to talking to his mother. Yes, he'd gotten the care package. No, he didn't need more socks and underwear. Yes, he was taking his vitamins. And could he please call her later?

There were some more *whan-whan-whan* sounds from the phone. He rolled his eyes heavenward before saying, "I love you, Mamma. Everything is fine. I'll call you in the morning."

After reassuring his mother he loved her forever, he hung up and offered a sheepish grin. "Sorry about that."

Whereas she could only shake her head. "Dude, that can't be healthy."

"She loves me."

Which was something Rilee couldn't comprehend. Even before she'd been shuffled into the foster care system, she'd not exactly had the best home life. Her mother discovered drugs when Rilee was young. By the time she was sixteen, she'd spent more times in government-sponsored care than with her parent. She never knew her dad.

"Your mother's love seems like a lot of work," she observed

"Some things are worth the effort. Let me help with the dishes."

She almost said no, fearful of the proximity, and yet as during the dinner-making, he was a perfect gentleman, not once even brushing a fingertip against her.

The fact she kept waiting for it to happen left her taut with tension. When the last dish was dried and put away, she fidgeted. She only had one comfortable chair. It would only fit two if one of them sat on the other. Not happening, which left the kitchen table again or her bed.

He grabbed his jacket and put it on before shoving his feet into his boots. "Thanks for having dinner with me."

Wait, was that it? He was just going to leave?

"It was delicious," she ventured, her hand dropping to her side, ready to grab her gun if needed. She had it leaning close by.

"I'm glad you enjoyed it. Next time, maybe I'll see if I can wrangle the stuff needed to make fettuccine carbonara."

"Isn't that the one with bacon? I love bacon." Her tone lilted.

"I'll give you anything you want, bella," was his gravelly reply.

"That supper made me sleepy. Time for me to hit

the sack." Not entirely true. She wasn't tired one bit. She tingled from head to toe.

Could he sense it? He stared at her hard and long enough she thought for sure he'd kiss her. Readied herself to say no for when he tried.

"Good night, bella." He left without making a move, and she went to bed disappointed.

Aching.

Wondering if she'd see him again. If she did, would she have the courage to steal a kiss?

CHAPTER 7

*M*ateo made himself leave in spite of the interest he scented. He walked away even though he wanted to stay.

He was barely out of sight of her cottage and he couldn't wait to see her again.

It was madness. One person shouldn't be able to consume his thoughts, and yet in a short time, she had. He couldn't have defined exactly what made her different than the rest.

Beauty scratched only the surface of it. He sensed a toughness that covered a vulnerability. The way she'd overcome adversity showed her courage and her unwillingness to give up. When he drew a smile, it was because he'd earned it. She didn't flirt outrageously or compliment him nonstop. She didn't do any of the things women usually did to get in his bed.

Heck, half the time, he wondered if she even perceived him in that way. He sure as hell saw her that way. Even now, as he leaned against the tree, if he closed his eyes, he could picture her, the soft lighting of the candles bathing her face in a gentle warmth, bringing out the flecks in her eyes. But it was her scent that truly stuck with him. A hint of the woods and a musk that was hers alone, teasing of arousal.

He'd wanted to kiss her before he left. Didn't dare. It was too soon. Wasn't it?

Given her skittish nature, he couldn't assume she'd welcome a kiss. How was a man supposed to ask a woman without ruining the moment?

What if she said no?

What if she said yes?

He hardened at the thought. It didn't take actually touching to know the chemistry would be there, explosive and heated. Once they started, it would end in passionate lovemaking. He'd kiss every inch of her. Worship and show her that he was a person she could trust with her life.

They could live happily ever after—

In a little shack in the middle of the woods.

He grimaced. While he liked the tranquility of it, he wasn't sure he saw himself being a hermit the rest of his life. But he also doubted she'd ever agree to leave. Meaning what?

Nothing, because he was getting way ahead of himself. She'd tolerated him for a few hours, which only meant he'd taken a step in the right direction. He still had his work cut out getting her to trust him. It would take a lot more than one pot of pasta to make her fall in love. Good thing his banishment gave him time to devote to wooing her.

A reprieve that ended the next day when his boss called—his real boss, Terrence, not the town alpha. "Good thing we moved you into place when we did."

A reminder that he hadn't ended up here by accident. Yes, he'd been caught on camera. Yes, he needed to lie low, and what better cover than to be sent with a plausible excuse to a place of interest?

Kodiak Point had a problem. Mainly, someone had recently taken an interest in the town and made inquiries on the dark web. Asked questions that set off all kinds of alarms with the council—those who watched over shifters.

"What's up, boss?" he asked, stepping outside of his motel room. There were fifteen rooms in total, each furnished with a bed, desk with chair, a small three-piece bathroom, a microwave, and mini fridge. The perfect bachelor pad. No wonder his mother worried.

"Target group is on the move and headed for an established camp about one hundred and forty-five clicks east of town."

The target group consisted of hunters, which they strongly suspected of poaching, but not your jungle-variety kind of animals. These poachers only went after a specific kind of prey—shifters—and had thus far done an excellent job with masking their identity. But even on the dark web, trails could be followed. "How many in the group?"

"A lot," was his boss's grim reply. "Seventeen by our count."

He let out a low whistle as he surveyed the sleepy town. "Do we know for sure they're hunting the town's residents?"

"No idea, although they are locked and loaded for bear."

One detail niggled at Mateo. "Aren't there two other winter camps closer than the one they're heading for?" He'd studied the file before coming out.

"There are, but the one they chose is prime ground for caribou hunting, which is their cover."

"Or it might be a legitimate trip with a few bad seeds trying to mix in." Mateo rubbed his chin. "You going to inform the Kodiak alpha?"

"Not yet. We don't need any accidents. We will continue to monitor the situation, and you should be on the lookout for newcomers. Anyone coming into town should be treated with caution. We're talking rubber gloves because you're worried about an infection and paranoid to the point you're stripping naked and scrubbing with a wire brush." Terrence sometimes had a way with words.

"Be careful. Got it."

He didn't have a problem with his orders, except for one thing.

Within the hour, he was knocking on Reid's office door because the reception desk was empty.

"Come in," the alpha called from inside. He wasn't

alone. Boris leaned against a wall, and a massively sized fellow sprawled in a chair.

The leader of Kodiak Point offered him a curt nod. "Mateo, glad you're here. I'd like you to meet Gene. He's my field strategist."

The man rolled a glance in his direction and grunted. It was a common thing among the men in Kodiak Point, many who'd served in the military together. His mother wouldn't let him enlist with the human armies, which was why he'd jumped at the chance when Terrence recruited him.

"I didn't realize you were having a meeting. I'll return later," Mateo said, ready to turn around.

"No. Stay. I have a feeling you can give us a hand with our situation. Apparently, we have some poachers camping nearby."

"You know about them." Stated not asked.

"And so do you," Reid said softly. "Isn't that why the council sent you here? Because they were aware these killers were coming?"

Mateo stared at Reid and then cast a glance at Boris, who smirked and drawled, "Did you really think we didn't have you checked out before you arrived? Your cover story was weak at best."

"I was under orders not to say anything."

"And you didn't, but I've been talking to your boss. Your secret is out and now that we all know, what are we going to do about it? I won't have my people harmed. Nor am I keen on the idea of those bastards hunting on our grounds," Reid stated.

"It's more problematic than that," Mateo said. "Because that group doesn't just contain regular human hunters. It's also got trophy poachers who collect our kind."

"Meaning we need to put out a warning. Nobody shifts or goes into the woods until further notice."

"For how long? The full moon is coming. The days are short. You can't expect everyone to stay cooped up for long," Boris reminded.

"I say we go in at night, and they have an accident." Gene's blunt solution.

Reid shook his head. "We can't kill them. Some of them are innocent, not to mention, all of them dying at once? People will notice."

"And? Perhaps we should send a message that hunting is wrong." Boris agreed with Gene.

"Now is not the time to draw attention."

"I think it's too late for that," Mateo remarked. "Everywhere you look—in the news, online, in social media—stories are popping up about our existence."

"Exactly, and in order for us to maintain any kind of peace, we can't be perceived as killing beasts."

"But it's okay for them to kill us?" Gene rolled out of his chair. "I'm not going to sit back while those fuckers hunt us down as trophies."

After that announcement, there was some arguing, but in the end, the alpha prevailed. No killing without proof. However, he did order Gene to recruit someone and take turns actively watching the group. Boris went off mumbling about strengthening town defenses.

Once they were gone, Reid glanced at Mateo and said, "Someone has to tell Rilee about this danger. She should think about moving into town for the next little bit."

"She won't like it," Mateo said.

"She won't," Reid agreed.

Being an idiot, Mateo volunteered to tell her.

CHAPTER 8

*S*he heard the snowmobile before she saw him. He parked it in front of her place, and she watched him approach from behind her curtains. Having spent the previous evening, and most of the night and this morning, thinking about him, wondering when she'd see him again, it was elating and terrifying to have him back in the flesh.

She didn't know what to make of him. Bold and borderline pushy one minute, sweet with a rakish teasing the next. He made her long for things she'd thought herself past wanting. He made her want him, which was why she didn't answer when he knocked.

As if that would stop him. "Really, Rilee? I know you're in there."

Shifters always knew. "Go away. I'm busy."

"Would it help if I said I brought a treat?"

Was he talking about himself? She shook her head. "Not interested."

"What's wrong, bella? I thought we were getting along."

They were, which was the problem. She was scared. Of him. Of how he made her feel.

Time to shove aside her fear. She opened the door. "Why must you be so stubborn? Don't you have other people you can harass?" she asked on a note of exasperation.

"None that I like."

A simple admission that warmed her. "Where's this treat you promised?"

"Tada!" He held up a can of peaches.

"I have the exact same tin in my cupboard."

He waggled it and offered a winsome smile. "What if I said I could bake them into the most delicious cake?"

"You did not ride all the way here to make me dessert."

"What makes you think I wouldn't? You are an excellent dinner companion."

"It's not even lunch."

"I'll bet you're excellent at the noon hour and for a snack too." He winked.

She flushed. "I really do have things to do."

He glanced around. "Yes, I can see how the gardening and farming might be time consuming this time of year."

Her lips flattened. "It's cleaning day."

"Actually, more like moving out. Congratulations. You're getting a rent-free room in town."

Her expression probably matched her stubbornness. "I am not moving out of my house." She went to slam the door, but he wedged his foot in the crack.

"You forgot to ask me the reason why you need to move back to town."

"Let me guess. It's dangerous for a woman all alone. It's far." She ticked off fingers.

"It is a bit of a distance," he agreed.

She lifted her chin. "If you think I'm living too far, don't visit."

"Never said too far. But that's not the problem. There are poachers to the east."

"And?" She tried to remain casual even as fear clenched her belly.

"And Reid ordered everyone to remain close to town and in their two-legged shape to avoid mishaps."

"No shifting. Got it."

"This isn't a joke, bella. You need to come back. Temporarily at least," he quickly added.

"This is my home. I'm safe here. Or are you now going to claim those poachers shoot people on sight?"

His lips flattened, no sign of the jovial Mateo in his face. "These aren't your garden-variety type. They hunt shifters."

That knot in her stomach got even tighter. "They'll never know what I am."

"Why are you arguing? I can smell your fear. You know staying here is wrong."

She did and bowed her head. Sighed. "I hate that motel. The rooms are like a prison."

"Get the room adjoining mine and we'll leave the door open, so it feels more like a sprawling bungalow."

She wrinkled her nose. "Not helping."

"What if I promise that I will turn this can of peaches into an upside-down cake that will make your toes curl?"

Eyeing his mouth, she wanted to ask for a different kind of treat. He caught her staring and winked. She blushed as she glanced away. "I'll go back to town with you, but not without my things. I'll pack while you fetch the trailer."

"That will take too long. We can strap a bag to the back."

She shook her head. "That will only be enough for a few days, and I get the feeling you're taking a week or more." She could see Mateo every day.

"Come with me for the ride."

"Don't be silly. I need to gather the things I want. As it is, you should bring some of the canned stuff back with you this trip so it doesn't freeze once the wood-stove goes out."

She helped him bring a few cases to strap to the rack on the back of the sled. He gave her a hard stare before saying, "I'll be back within the hour with a trailer. Be ready."

She nodded and listened as the motor faded then got to work, filling a duffel with her clothes and personal effects. Then she packed a box with some books. Another stack was of the food that wouldn't survive freezing.

During that time, the sky darkened as clouds rolled in on strong, gusty winds. Fat snowflakes began to fall as she finished closing up the cottage, shuttering the interior window covers, making her bed. Then she sat and waited. Fell asleep, which might be why she never heard Mateo returning, only the hard knock on the door.

Half awake, she flew to the portal and opened it, momentarily blinded by the snow that swept in. It clung to her lashes, and she blinked.

Then gaped at the baklava-covered face. Utterly surprised by the stranger's appearance, she didn't notice the gun until it was too late.

CHAPTER 9

The snow began not long after Mateo got the sledge hitched to the snowmobile. He'd wasted a good forty-five minutes waiting for it rather than take the much smaller pod. The sledge had high walls and a tarp stretched over the top that would protect her things. He wasted another few minutes loading a few emergency supplies, not liking the look of the sky.

Boris showed up just as he finished filling the gas tank. "Weather's about to get rough. You might want to wait it out."

"Rilee's alone out there."

"Tucked tight in her cabin. She'll be fine. You on the other hand…" The up-and-down glance let Mateo clearly understand what Boris thought of the city slicker.

The moose man wasn't entirely wrong. Mateo hadn't done much work in the deep north in winter.

Add in a storm and things could get downright treacherous. However, a nagging unease wouldn't let him sit safe in his motel waiting out the vicious wind.

"I need to go. I've got supplies in the sled just in case." Rations, sleeping bag, and, in his pocket, fruit cake, courtesy of his mother.

Boris gave him a hard stare then clapped him on the back. "If you get turned around, dig yourself a burrow and hunker until the worst of it passes."

He wouldn't be doing shit until he found Rilee.

The visibility didn't prove the greatest, the storm and the short window of daylight making it dark outside, even gloomier in the forest. The beam of his headlight was the only thing illuminating his path, speckled with falling snow. The rapidly multiplying flakes thickened until he could see nothing, meaning he had to slow down lest he slam headlong into a tree. He'd probably survive, but it would hurt like a bitch.

The unease that started in town only increased as he realized he no longer knew if he was heading in the right direction. Slowing his sled, he took a moment to shove up his sleeve and poke at his watch. Built-in GPS would show him his location on a map. If the satellite could read the signal.

From behind his goggles, he glared upwards at the storm-heavy sky. He couldn't tell north from south. Nor was there any sign of a path. He'd been travelling more than twenty minutes at this point. Had he gone right past her place? Fuck, for all he knew, it was within spitting distance. He'd begun to wonder if he'd have to take Boris's advice and burrow under a heap of snow when he heard it even over the hum of his engine.

A sharp crack.

A gunshot!

At that point, all reason left him. He flipped off the machine and jumped to the ground. It only took two steps for him to realize the snow would slow him.

He shed his clothes and quickly stuffed them under the tarp for the sledge. He was shivering, and his balls turtled by the time he shifted.

The pain of reshaping had him arching, but not crying out, because he'd done this so many times. He knew what came after the agony. Euphoria.

While Mateo enjoyed the pleasures of two legs and flesh, there was something about being his tiger that brought things down to a simpler level.

Primitive, and yet all the more enjoyable for it. The snow no longer proved a deterrent, his wide paws made for this kind of weather. The Amur tigers weren't just known for being the biggest felines; they had manes more useful and warm than a lion's, cuffs of fur around their legs, and an ability to see in the dark that made them excellent hunters.

Who needed a GPS when instinct never steered him wrong?

While he didn't hear a second gunshot, engine noise did rumble in the distance. He made haste and only slowed as he spotted lights amidst the falling snow and branches. Time to get higher.

He climbed a tree and stretched out along a thick branch and inched until he could glimpse Rilee's hut. The front door gaped wide open. A man stood in it, dressed in camouflage snow gear, his features concealed by a baklava. He gestured to his similarly covered companions and shouted over the chugging of the snowmobiles parked out front, one of them tethered to a covered trailer. Big enough to stuff a body? He couldn't be sure. Or was Rilee still inside her home?

Two of the guys jammed dark tinted helmets on their heads before they hopped onto the snowmobile with the covered trailer. They turned around in the clearing by her place, preparing to leave. The remaining fellow moved toward the other sled.

A stupider man would have rushed in. A smart one noticed the weapons worn by the three men. Two handguns. A rifle. And another rifle strapped to a machine. Three against one and a woman to protect.

Not the worst odds. Hitting the ground, he began to weave through the trees, moving at an angle that would intercept the moving sled.

The *whoosh* proved move of a feeling than a sound that drew his attention. Despite the falling snow and trees in the way, he saw her cottage ablaze.

The urge to race and check inside hit him hard. What if he was wrong and she wasn't in the trailer?

If he'd fucked up, then he was already too late. He prayed his gut didn't lead him astray.

The snowmobiles couldn't move very fast in this weather, which worked to his advantage. He managed to get ahead and let the first machine, with its single rider, chug past and waited for the one with cargo.

From his hiding spot, he timed his leap and knocked the driver clean. He couldn't stop the shouting of his companion though. He had to work fast. He leaped into the snow and landed atop the driver. Having caught the man by surprise, he had no time to pull a weapon, and he had no time to fool around.

The helmet made it tricky, but a human was no match for a tiger.

Crunch. The first threat stopped moving, but the second had time to arm himself. *Bang.*

Bang.

Fire sliced over a shoulder blade as a bullet skimmed too close.

"Rawr!"

The next shot went wild, the man panicking but, worse than that, drawing attention. It wouldn't be long before the other rider came back to help.

The snow helped hide Mateo, the white shit clinging to his fur and whiskers, concealing him until the moment he pounced. The gun was no more.

At that point, he had two choices. Hop naked on that sled and ride for safety, in a storm. Probably crash and freeze a bunch of important body parts off.

Or, he could do the unexpected. He grabbed the key on the sled with his teeth and shut it off, plunging them in pure darkness. It would make them harder to spot.

The strap on the trailer gave way when he grabbed it with his teeth. He flipped off the cover, and if a tiger could have sighed, he would have, as he perceived Rilee within, wrapped in a blanket.

He heard a voice and glanced over at the body quickly accumulating snow. The helmet was talking and not getting a reply. He nosed Rilee, willing her to wake up.

She grumbled in her sleep.

"Rawr." He tried to nudge her awake, but she didn't stir.

Fuck.

He heard the hum of the other snowmobile. He couldn't stick around. Shit was about to get cold. Despite the danger to his dangling parts, he shifted. He took the blanket she was wrapped in and swaddled it around his naked shoulders, before scooping her into his arms and tucking her close. Then he took off, the direction not as important as getting her away from the enemy.

The good news was the snow would cover his tracks. But at the same time, he'd left the enemy behind.

An asshole who'd tried to take Rilee.

He didn't go far. Didn't have to because of the thicket he encountered. A previous snowfall that partially had melted and then froze had welded the branches at the top, meaning once he shoved in through the middle, by cracking a ton of small branches, he could make a temporary nest, where he deposited Rilee. Tucked that blanket around her.

Then, once more wearing his fur, he went hunting.

CHAPTER 10

*S*he shivered. *Cold. Always so cold. It didn't help he'd finally returned to taunt her.*

It had been many days since she'd had to deal with his torture. Blessed relief. While she hated the cage, it provided a form of safety from the kicks and the punches. The cigarette burns. All the things he did to try and force her to his will.

He raged because she wouldn't change for him on demand. It took only once, one stupid time, to realize what a mistake that was. She'd given in, appeared as herself, crouched in that cage, naked and clinging to the bars, pleading. "Please, you have to let me go."

He replied, "So it is true. Do you know what kind of prize you are?"

The guy she knew as Shayne stood outside her cage once again, fingers tucked in his pockets and not poking at her through the bars. Apparently, he'd learned since the time he'd needed seventeen stitches to close the gash. She'd learned, too, with the seventeen lashes meted by a silver barbed whip. The whip hung on the wall behind him, as did the other tools that could inflict pain.

What Shayne never understood was she preferred the pain of refusing his wishes to the apathy if she gave in. She would never let him win. Never give him what he wanted.

Shifter babies. His and hers. He'd discovered to his annoyance that implantation using human sperm wouldn't work while she was in her lynx shape. So long as she stayed an animal, he could do nothing about it.

"*I see you'd still rather be a beast in a cage,*" *he stated, as if she chose to be imprisoned.* "*How much longer are you going to be stubborn? Used to be you didn't mind my touch.*"

That was before she knew him to be a monster. Before the betrayals. Even the name she knew him by was false. She bared a fang.

"*Still feisty. Glad to see it because I got an offer for you.*"

As if she'd take any deal. She growled.

He laughed. "*Not that kind of offer. Someone wants you. Very badly. Even more than I do. And they're willing to pay for it. They're also not as bothered as I am when it comes to the whole animal-fucking thing. Not to mention, he's already got a lynx stud waiting for you. I hear he's hoping for a whole litter of kittens. You'll get to be a mom. What do you say to that?*"

She threw herself at the bars of her cage, only to yelp. The electricity running through them sent her to the dirty floor.

"*Rilee. Rilee. Rilee,*" *Shayne cajoled, kneeling so he could gloat in her face.* "*You should have been nicer to me. Not that it matters anymore. You had your chance. My friend has promised me pick of the first litter. I'm thinking I'd like a girl. One I'll raise to be obedient."*

If she'd had anything in her stomach, she might have vomited. But she'd not eaten in days and, by the next morning, was passed out in her cage. There was consternation among her handlers. No one wanted to be the one to tell the boss his prized lynx had died.

It made them clumsier than usual. Less careful as they opened her cage door to check on her vitals.

She sliced the jugular of the first attendant, effectively killing him before they realized she feigned her unconsciousness. By the time one of them ran to sound an alarm, she was out of her cage and pouncing.

She'd had time to figure out how she'd escape because she knew she'd only get one chance.

One chance to live, which was why she closed her ears to the screams, shut her eyes to the blood. The bullet wound that skimmed her as she scrambled up and over the gate of his estate eventually healed.

The anxiety never left.

Because she'd always worried one day she'd open the door and he'd be there.

Waiting to bring her back.

And then he was there. Damning her. Laughing. "I'm back, Rilee."

"No!" The word whispered on her lips as she woke suddenly, still caught in her nightmare, where she opened the door to her cottage and encountered those eyes. The eyes she'd never forget.

Her biggest fear come to life.

Shayne had found her.

And the very thought froze her.

She kept still to assess her situation. She wasn't in her bed, and yet she felt warm and comfortable. A blanket covered her. Her blanket, she realized in the dim gray light, and yet the real heat came from the furry body lying wedged beside her. Her breathing quickened.

Then stilled completely as the beast snuffled against her. As her heart slowed its racing, she managed to filter past the panic to realize who the giant feline was.

"Mateo?"

He chuffed, and she shifted to see in the dimness the massive tiger keeping her from feeling the cold. Handsome as a man, even more gorgeous as his cat. And of a fearsome size.

"How? What happened?" She struggled to rise, only to hyperventilate as she realized they were in a tight box of some sort. Walls pressed in on her. Closed her in. Trapped her.

I'm in a coffin buried alive!

"Shh. Bella." His voice surrounded her, steady and reassuring. The fur gone, leaving flesh.

"Where are we? Are we dead?" Her voice wavered.

"Do I feel dead to you?" was his dry reply. Still just as hot in the flesh. "We're taking cover in the sledge. The storm was too ferocious for me to drive us back to town."

Indeed, she could hear it whistling outside. "What happened?"

"You tell me."

Explain how she'd stupidly opened the door to her enemy. How she'd been taken off guard. She should have woken in a cage. Which could only mean... "You came for me."

"I'll always come for you, bella."

Relief emerged in tears, and she buried her face against his chest, body shaking as the fear took her. He wrapped her in his arms and hugged her, murmuring reassurance.

Slowly, the panic eased, and she managed to drag in deep breaths. "I'm okay now," she managed to whisper.

"I'm not," he admitted. "I should have never left you alone." Guilt soaked the admission.

"You couldn't have known. But I did. I knew one day he'd come back to find me."

For a moment, he stiffened. "The kidnapping was targeted?"

She nodded before softly saying, "He found me."

"The man who held you prisoner." Stated because he'd obviously been told. It wasn't as if her ordeal were a secret.

"I should have known I'd never be safe."

"Don't you dare even think that. You don't have to worry about those fuckers coming after you again." His vehemence enveloped her. Then more ominously, "I took care of it."

He didn't say he killed them. He didn't have to. The very fact should have sent her fleeing his violent arms, but instead, she smiled. "My hero." She shifted to see his face in the gloom. "Thank you."

He stared at her, his expression smoldering, and he sounded strangled as he said, "You're welcome. Want some fruitcake?"

Turned out, he'd come slightly prepared. Under the tarp, with the wind whistling outside, they dined on MRIs topped off with his mom's fruitcake, fruity and nutty. She was warm inside the sledge, the walls high enough they could move about a little bit, especially once he sat up, his head pushing the tarp and raising the ceiling a bit. He'd managed to dress in the clothes that he'd had the foresight to tuck inside the sledge.

"How long do we need to stay here?" she asked.

"Do you know your way to town in a storm?"

She shook her head.

"Then I guess we'll have to wait it out."

"And do what?" she asked.

Talk, apparently. He regaled her with more stories about his childhood. Even told her about his father dying in the line of duty.

"He was a good cop. And a great dad," he said, his tone somber. "My mom was crushed when he died."

"Which is why you're super close."

"Yeah." He shrugged. "I'm all she has. You know how it is."

She didn't, but given he'd spilled his guts, she had to spill hers. "I never knew my dad. My mom wasn't the type to stick around with one guy. Grass is greener and all that. She also wasn't the type to want to take care of a kid. It cramped her style."

He frowned. "Children are a blessing."

"Unless your boyfriend starts eyeballing your daughter and you feel old. Then I guess it's okay to sell her secrets." Too late she clamped her mouth shut.

"Your mother told someone what you are?" Shock filled the words.

"She never understood why I was different. To her I was a freak. Heck, I thought there was something wrong with me until I met others."

He sounded sad as he said, "I'm sorry you had a shitty childhood. You deserved better, bella."

"Kind of my own fault for sticking around." A bitter laugh. "I mean I knew she hated me; I just didn't know how much." Not until she woke in that cage and Shayne, a guy she'd briefly dated but who proved too intense—not to mention she couldn't stomach the fact he boasted about his poaching—bragged about how her mother had sold him the information about what she was. A mother who betrayed her daughter for drug money.

"You're sure he's dead?" she asked, suddenly desperate for reassurance. Opening that door, seeing *his* face… She trembled. She had to be sure the nightmare was finally over.

"After I killed the two dragging you off, I hunted down the third. They're not coming back."

Three people dead because of her. One of them had

to be Shayne. As for the other two... They should have made better choices.

She uttered a shuddering sigh. He was gone.

She didn't have to be scared anymore. And she had Mateo to thank.

It was the wrong time. Wrong place. But she still cupped his cheeks and kissed him. Lightly. Worried the panic might rise to crush her.

When it didn't, she kissed him again and again, soft pecks that turned into a deeper embrace. He dragged her into his lap, and despite her layers, she felt his erection. But the most surprising and welcome thing of all, desire.

She squirmed as she sought to straddle him, suddenly impatient. He groaned against her mouth as her hot tongue slid against his.

"We really should be thinking of ways we can get back to town."

"Later," she muttered. She'd come face to face with her worst nightmare last night, and it proved to be the epiphany that made her realize she'd been living—no, she'd been existing—in a state of fear, waiting for that day.

Wasted her life. Missed out on so many things, like the pleasure that could be had with a man.

"Touch me," she asked.

"Are you sure?" he mumbled against her lips.

"I think so." Only to add more firmly, "Yes."

His fingers found the edge of her sweater and skimmed under, tugging at her thermal undershirt before finding her smooth flesh.

She shivered, not in cold but at the sensation of his rougher fingertips abrading her skin. Touching her. She leaned back that he might tug her shirt upward, baring her breasts to his view.

When he paused, she grabbed his head and pushed it toward the budding tip.

He needed no more invitation. He took it into his mouth and sucked, the warmth of it drawing a groan.

His hands cupped her breasts, pushing them together as he lavished them with attention, drawing gasping moans. When he let his fingers wander, she helped by getting on her knees that he might unbutton her pants and slide his hand in to cup her.

"I want to taste you," was the murmured plea against her flesh.

Not the easiest thing to do in their bower with its blanket and tarp but she managed to lie down. He tugged her pants down enough that he could get to the treasure between her thighs.

At the first lick, she arched. By the second and third, she was thrashing. His tongue had a slight roughness to it that drove her wild. And when he slid a pair of fingers into her, she rode his hand, rode it until she came, crying out at the unexpected pleasure of it.

Reaching for him, trying to drag him closer. "I need you."

"Later," he murmured against her, still licking and stroking until she came again, even harder.

When she finally recovered her breath, it was to find herself wrapped in his arms, with him—

"Are you purring?"

"Yup."

"Big cats don't purr."

"This tiger does. But only for the right woman," he added, giving her a squeeze.

"The storm doesn't look like it's lightening again. Rather than spend another night in the sled, maybe we should try and find my house. We'll get a fire going in the stove, and you can make me that peach dessert you promised," she suggested as her stomach rumbled.

He stiffened, and his voice was a low rumble as he said, "We can't, bella. Your house is gone. They torched it before leaving."

"Gone?" she whispered. What of her things? Her books? Her clothes? For a moment, she almost cried, and then she remembered the important thing.

She was alive. This wouldn't be first time she started over. "Guess I'd better hope they still have that room for me at the motel."

"Or you could stay with me."

CHAPTER 11

*T*oo much. Too soon. He should have kept his mouth shut. A hint of panic lit Rilee's gaze. Since he didn't know how to counter it, he kissed her.

And kept kissing her. But rather than make love to her again, he held her close, listening to the wind as it died down that night.

When the skies cleared, his GPS activated, and he received a flurry of texts. His mother's being the most strident.

A sleepy Rilee said, "She must be freaking. You didn't call her two nights in a row."

Actually, the more ominous thing was the lack of messages since the previous afternoon. He fired a quick one to his mother that simply said, "Alive. Busy. Will call when I can." Then to Reid, "Have Rilee. Snow has stopped. Will see if sled still running. Trouble."

He didn't wait for a reply. It was time for them to move. But not before he kissed Rilee again.

She ducked her head. "Guess it's time to return to the real world."

Was she as reluctant as he was? Once they arrived, he knew they wouldn't have much time together because the attack changed everything. However, he didn't say any of that to Rilee because, after the intimacy they'd shared, it wasn't how he wanted to start the day. They shoved their way out of their sled tent.

The world beyond remained mostly dark, the dawn only starting, meaning it was already late morning. He'd slept longer than expected.

Fresh snow coated everything, including the snowmobile, which was buried. The sledge they'd sheltered in was buried as well, which kept them insulated but would not allow them an easy departure.

When digging only buried it further, he had to admit defeat. "We're going to have to walk."

He sounded so unhappy. She put her hand on his arm. "It's fine. Let's get layered up." Her kidnappers had at least somewhat dressed her for the elements, meaning she had boots and a coat, but no insulated pants.

He had full gear, but neither had snowshoes. Every step they took, they sank. Thigh deep in some places.

She grumbled, "This will take us forever."

"I'll send another message to Reid."

She sighed. "Please don't. Then I'll have to listen to a lecture on how he warned me living out here put me at risk."

"Then I guess there's only one thing to do. Let's see this infamous lynx." He flicked snow at her.

The only real solution but for one problem. "I hate shifting in snow," she grumbled as she stripped.

Whereas he quite enjoyed the show. In the confines of the sledge, he'd barely been able to see her, and he only got the quickest of glimpses before she turned into her cat. By the time she finished transforming, he'd also shed his clothing and was sniffing at the lovely lynx, with her gray and white coloring, fur as thick, maybe thicker even, than his own. Her tail was a short snappy thing. She uttered a playful yip before sprinting off.

It was on!

They raced through the trees, the silence broken only by the cracking of branches snapping under the weight of the snow and the occasional whoosh of snow as it fell in a clump. The crisp smell invigorated the lungs but was soon overshadowed by that of something burnt. Apparently, he had overshot his destination the night before. The shell of the cottage saw the lynx pausing for a gander before she ran off again, and since she knew these woods better than him, he followed.

Just outside of town, they ran into Boris patrolling the edge, sitting on a snowmobile, rifle in his lap.

He took one look at them and said, "Ah fuck. What happened?"

Given they were both cats it sounded like, "Rawr. Meow."

Boris grunted. "No idea what that's supposed to be.

Let's get some pants on you both and get you over to Reid's office. You can borrow some of Jan's stuff," he offered.

Only Rilee shook her head and sidled closer to Mateo, which had Boris raising both brows.

"Oh. In that case then, figure it out, but make it quick. I can probably give you a half-hour, but don't take any longer or shit might get ugly."

A cryptic statement. Running down the recently plowed street, Mateo led them to the motel, where he had to change shapes and spend a naked second outside to open the door to his motel room. Never locked. What would they steal?

She stepped in and shifted, head ducked as if suddenly shy. He wouldn't let her retreat from him, not after the progress they made. He shut the door behind him.

"Let's get you into a hot shower."

"Oh, that sounds heavenly!" Her expression brightened.

"I gotta ask, what did you do at your cottage to bathe?"

"In the summer, there's a lake nearby. But in the winter, I melt snow into a tub and sponge wash mostly. Unless I come to town. Then I have a shower at Jan and Boris's place."

Turning on the taps, he stepped back to wait while the water warmed. Then he gave in to temptation and grabbed her ass. She glanced at him over her shoulder.

"Checking it for ripeness?"

"It's too perfect to resist."

"Liar."

"What's that supposed to mean?"

"I'm well aware I have a big butt."

"I happen to think your ass is perfect."

"It's too wide."

"Just right." He squeezed it again. "If you only knew how many times I've imagined you bent over with this perfect ass up in the air, you wouldn't argue."

She didn't argue, and the scent of her arousal filled the tight space. Her eyelids dropped to half-mast, and she licked her lips. Not immune to compliments. Good to know.

When the water ran if not hot, at least semi warm, he stepped into the shower and held out his hand in invitation.

"I don't think there's enough room."

"Get in here, bella."

She joined him in the tight cubby, the water hitting them and trying to find a way between their tightly pressed bodies.

The soap hung from a rope, and he lathered his hands before he ran them over her luscious body. Big ass, like fuck. She might be short, but she had an hourglass shape that was all woman. His woman.

She might not have said it aloud yet, but the very fact she stood in this shower with him was all he needed.

The feel of her silky-smooth skin teased him. Hardened him. He turned her so that she had her back to him and ran soapy hands over her breasts, rolling her nipples until they puckered into tight peaks. He tugged them and drew a moan. Her head tilted back, leaning on him, her eyes closed, her lips parted.

But the sexiest thing of all? How she trusted him.

He slid a hand between her thighs to stroke her slick folds and found her wet already. He dropped to his knees, face level with her pubes. A glance upward showed her gazing down at him, eyes heavy with desire. Arousal roared through him.

"You are so fucking beautiful, bella."

"Show me," was her husky murmur.

It was almost enough to make him come. Spreading her thighs and lifting one to hang over his shoulders, giving him better access, he buried his face in her sex. Enveloped by her womanly scent. Decadent and mouthwatering.

He parted her nether lips with his tongue and tasted her sweetness. He lapped at her, quick flicks of his tongue against her that had her hips rocking in motion, but it was the latch of his lips on her clit that drew a cry.

She had a hold of his head, fingers digging into his scalp. A painful grip that only heightened his arousal.

He gripped her ass to hold her in place as she trembled with each stroke and suck. As her cries turned into breathless mewls, he knew she was close to coming, and he growled against her, a soft vibration that sent a shiver through her.

Mine. All mine.

He had no doubt on that score. He licked her faster, wanting her to come on his tongue, but she gasped. "I want to feel you inside me."

The shock almost killed him. He would have been content to pleasure her. He was ready to wait if needed.

She yanked on him, pulling him upright and grabbing his cheeks to drag him in for a kiss.

"Are you sure?" he murmured against her lips, his cock throbbing where it was trapped between their bodies.

"I'm tired of hiding. Tired of not living." She peered at him through wet lashes. "I want you."

She made no other demand. No promise, but it was enough for him. The shower was tight, but he flipped her around. She placed her palms on the shower wall, which tilted her butt.

He took his time, sliding his hand between her legs, working her clit until she pushed against him, murmuring, "Stop teasing."

He rubbed the head of cock against her, slowly pushing in, the tightness of her driving him wild. But he was careful because of his size.

But she was done being careful. She bent over farther and shoved herself onto him, driving him deep. They both cried out and stilled. Him with his fingers digging into her hips. Her taut, her sex the only thing pulsing.

"Fuck. Fuck. Fuck." It was his mantra as he slowly withdrew and then slid back in. The pleasure was almost too much. He clenched tight, determined to not come until he felt her climaxing.

Soon, going slow wasn't an option. He found himself thrusting into her, over and over, each jab drawing a sharp cry from her and then a panted, "Yes. Yes. Yes."

He wouldn't be able to hold on much longer, and then thankfully he didn't have to. With a strangled moan, she shattered around his cock, her slick muscles squeezing him tight, binding him to her. And then he came, marking her with his seed. He thrust one final time deep inside. Their bodies pulsed in time.

When he slipped out, he turned and pulled her into his arms, holding her against him, feeling her breathing slow as she nuzzled his chest.

"That was..." She paused.

"Epic?" he supplied.

"Will it always be like that?" she asked, looking up at him.

"Actually, I predict it will get even better."

He basked in the smile on her lips. A smile that, despite everything, didn't waver as they dressed. She didn't have anything clean, so she had to borrow from him, the long johns tight on him but loose on her. The sweater he gave her hung down almost to her knees. She looked sexy as hell in it.

"Fuck meeting with Reid. Let's stay here for the day."

"He has to be told what happened." But said with a pleased smile.

"I know. But once we're done, I am stripping you naked and worshipping every inch of your body."

"I'd like that." She blushed and ducked her head.

The thirty minutes Boris gave them were almost up, meaning it was time. They layered on their snow gear, ready to walk, only to find a side-by-side parked out front, keys in the ignition.

She sat beside him, clinging tight to the oh-shit bar as he did a few donuts, her laughter music to his ears. Much more pleasant than the familiar screech that erupted the moment he walked into Reid's office.

"My bambino! I was so worried."

CHAPTER 12

"*M*y baby. You're alive."

There was no doubt in Rilee's mind this was Mateo's mother.

A normal person would have blanched, perhaps run, but not Mateo. He smiled. "Mamma! What are you doing here?" He wagged a finger as if she were naughty.

And the grown woman giggled.

Whatever image she might have created in her mind, it didn't match the reality. Mamma, as Mateo called Mrs. Ricci, didn't look old enough to have a son his age. Sure, she had some streaks of gray in her dark hair, but they lent her an elegance and maturity that was enhanced by a voluptuous figure wearing a knit sweater that hugged her curves.

On a chair next to her was a brand-new parka, startling red in color, a knitted hat with matching mittens, and scarf. Obviously, a family who liked wool, because she couldn't help but notice how many sweaters were stuffed in his dresser at the motel.

Mateo hugged his mother. Like seriously grabbed her and lifted her for a shake and squeeze. "I can't believe you're here."

"I had to come. When you didn't call, I got worried."

He frowned. "That doesn't explain how you got here so fast. Especially since the storm didn't end until a few hours ago."

"Because she bribed someone to drive through unsafe conditions," Reid muttered.

That drew a snapping glare that was the complete opposite of her expression when dealing with Mateo. Rilee found it fascinating to watch. It was as if Mrs. Ricci became a whole new person. "Perhaps I wouldn't have gone to extreme measures if you'd taken my phone call seriously. I advised you my son was in trouble."

"And as I told you, he was fine. Visiting a, um, friend," Reid stammered. Then shrugged apologetically at Rilee.

"Actually, he saved my life," Rilee stated.

That dropped a few jaws.

"What happened?" Reid hastened to ask.

Boris straightened. "Did you have some trouble?"

She would have told them, but Mateo smoothly intervened. "Rilee's place burned down during the storm, so we had to take shelter in the sledge."

"Oh shit. Sorry, Rilee." Reid looked and sounded sympathetic.

"It's just stuff," she mumbled.

"If you need anything, you come talk to me or Jan," Boris insisted.

"I'll give you a full accounting as soon as I get my mother settled," Mateo said, rather than explaining how it burned. Apparently, he didn't want his mother hearing the details.

"Such a good boy thinking of me. But no need. They've loaned me a lovely home with a kitchen that is barely adequate, but one must make do." Mrs. Ricci was a martyr.

"When did you get here?" Mateo asked.

"Only minutes after you left on a rescue mission. Always a hero," Mrs. Ricci said with pride.

"You shouldn't have gone through the trouble. I'm fine," Mateo said.

"Now you are, but at the time, you could have been dead in a ditch."

"There are no ditches here, Mamma."

"Perhaps not but there are other dangers." The quickly slewed gaze lasered in on Rilee. "Such as malnutrition. I saw on our last video call that you were looking a bit thin. Can't have my boy starving. I brought a few things with me."

"A few? You brought an entire kitchen sink," muttered Boris.

Surely he was joking?

"You can't expect me to fill a proper pasta pot with a regular faucet." Mateo's mama sniffed with disdain.

While Mateo might have a soft spot for his mother,

he also apparently had a breaking point. "I haven't lost any weight. How can I? I've only been gone a week."

"Longest week of my life," she exaggerated, and Rilee had to bite her lip.

It really was entertaining to watch. It also made her a tad bit jealous. She'd never been loved by anyone that much.

"Remember that conversation we had about respecting my space?"

"Blah, blah, something about I wasn't to bother you when you're working." She clasped her hands, and her innocent expression held a hint of slyness. "You specifically told me your relocation to Kodiak Point wasn't work related. Surely you didn't lie to your mother?" She actually batted her lashes.

"Don't do this."

"Do what? Wonder if my sweet bambino, the most important thing in the world, trusts his own mother after she went through thirty-seven hours of labor because of his giant head?"

"You know I trust you," he said.

"But you don't love me anymore." She sniffed.

"You're being ridiculous, Mamma."

"Then why don't you want me to visit?" Neatly done. She'd cornered him, and he knew it.

Mateo groaned. "You know I can't tell you when I'm undercover."

The word brought a hint of panic. Wait? Had Mateo lied about who he was?

She took a step away from him.

Despite the drama with his mother, he noticed. "I'm here for work, but it had nothing to do with you, bella. I swear."

"Then why are you here?" she asked.

"Because of those poachers." The ones he'd tried to tell her about.

His mother didn't appreciate losing his attention and hotly exclaimed, "I knew you were in danger! I told these people"—she cast a disparaging glare at Reid and the others—"that you were in trouble. But did they listen? No, they delayed sending out a search party for my baby boy."

"You saw that blizzard! We had to wait for the storm to die down," exclaimed Reid.

"My bambino could have died while you stayed safe in your dens," Mrs. Ricci said with a sniff.

"Mamma, you're being crazy. I didn't die."

"But you could have. And whose fault would that be?" The fearsome gaze finally landed on Rilee and stayed. Mrs. Ricci pursed her lips. "I don't think we've been introduced. I'm Tanya Ricci. And you are?"

"Rilee." She didn't give a last name because she'd decided when in that cage that she only belonged to herself. No family. No name. Just the me, myself, and I.

"Why are you wearing the sweater I made my son?" Mrs. Ricci asked pointedly.

"Because she lost all her clothes when her house burned down."

"That's convenient," Mrs. Ricci drawled.

"Yes, because I totally wanted to lose all my things

and have to wear oversized scratchy castoffs." The sweater wasn't actually rough, but she did enjoy the pursed lips.

"Be nice, Mamma." Mateo placed a hand on Rilee's lower back, offering her support. She might need it. If mama tiger attacked, it would get ugly.

Mrs. Ricci's gaze turned assessing. "You left in a storm to help this girl?"

"Yup."

He said nothing more. She could see his mother was dying to ask but holding back.

Which was when Reid finally interrupted. "Perhaps you'd like to take this reunion elsewhere while I talk to Rilee about the fire."

"I should be present for that. Mamma and I can chat later," Mateo declared, and for just a second, she expected Mrs. Ricci to protest.

Instead, she lifted her chin. "Since I'm obviously not wanted here, I shall leave."

"Don't be like that, Mamma. I just need to talk to the alpha, and then I'll come see you. How else will I get fresh cookies?"

His mother tsked. "You and your cookies. Don't think I'm going to bake for you now."

"But I thought you said I looked skinny." Mateo turned her words against her.

"Cookies are bad for you," Rilee declared. "Fattening. How about I make you a salad later?" She did it on purpose, and Mrs. Ricci fell for it.

"Salad? That's for herbivores." There was scorn in the reply. "I shall make a roast."

"With dumplings?" he insisted. "I need them."

Not want, need, and his mother nodded. "And pudding for dessert. I'll need to get started right away."

"Do you need an escort to your place?" he asked.

His mother managed a tart, "Are you implying this town isn't safe? I should have known. Bears tend to be slackers in the winter."

Reid gaped.

Before he had to reply, Rilee stepped in. "The town is actually very safe. I'm sure your son is more concerned that someone of your age might find navigating the icy streets challenging." She smiled sweetly.

Mrs. Ricci's gaze narrowed. "I'm in the prime of my life."

"I hope you brought your vitamin supplements along with the kitchen sink. Strong bones are important as you get older."

There was a lot of coughing going on, and Mrs. Ricci's eyes flashed, but not with anger, more like intrigue. And challenge. "I brought everything I could need, including the ingredients for bambino's favorite foods. He loves my cooking."

It was bad, so wrong and bad, but she couldn't resist saying, "And you taught him well. I can't wait until he cooks for me again..." She closed her eyes and moaned.

"He cooked for you." A low statement.

Reid coughed. "Um, I think I need to check on something with Boris."

"Yeah. Like now." The pair left.

But Mrs. Ricci didn't seem bothered she'd essentially kicked the alpha out of his own office. She glared at Mateo. "Do you want to tell me something?"

"Not really."

"Perhaps you want to explain why she's wearing your clothes and reeks of you."

Amongst shapeshifters, scent wasn't something that could be controlled. Rilee did her best with the extract she made that left her smelling like pine cleaner, but she'd lost that perfume. And they had just showered together. Heck, she hoped their plans were still a go for later that night. He had promised.

Rilee lifted her chin and said, "We are dating." The moment the words left her mouth, she regretted them. His mother already appeared to hate her. Which meshed with the stories he'd regaled her with of disliking anyone he dated. According to him, she found things to pick apart. Reasons why they weren't good enough for her son.

So when Mrs. Ricci turned that assessing gaze on her, she feared the worst. "You are dating? As in a couple?"

She nodded, hoping Mateo would forgive the little lie. Then again, he'd claimed they were mates.

Mrs. Ricci looked at Mateo as if to confirm.

"She's important to me, Mamma." He actually said it, and the warmth inside her had her smiling at him.

He winked.

Mrs. Ricci's glance bounced between them, and when her mouth opened, Rilee braced herself.

"You're too skinny. I will feed you. Dinner will be served at five."

And then Mrs. Ricci marched out.

Rilee stared for a moment before muttering, "What just happened?"

"I don't know. She's never offered to cook for one of my girlfriends before." His bemused expression didn't help.

"Think she'll try and poison me?" was her dubious query.

"I hope not." Not the most reassuring thing he could have said.

Reid and Boris chose that moment to return and spent a few minutes teasing Mateo about his mother. He bore it with good will and, despite his mother's overbearingly tight apron strings, was not the least bit resentful.

A part of her wondered if she'd feel as benevolent if someone tried to smother her in that much affection.

Once the joking ended, they reported what happened, mainly the fact she'd opened the door to her worse enemy. The man she'd come to Kodiak Point to escape.

Despite having killed her attackers, Mateo had some concerns. "I want to know how he knew Rilee would be here. Because I highly doubt she's taking pictures and posting them on social media."

She shook her head. "I don't even own a camera. As

for Shayne finding out? I never had a chance to ask. He shot me with a few tranquilizers the moment I opened the door."

Reid growled. "Fucking bastard."

Whereas Boris snapped, "You opened the door without checking who it was first?

She shrugged and ducked her head, her cheeks heating as she muttered, "I thought it was Mateo."

He reached for her hand and squeezed it. "Which is my fault. I got caught up in town and then went right past your place in the storm."

"I can't believe they went after her so brazenly. You're sure they're dead?" Reid asked bluntly.

He nodded. "Three men. Two sleds."

"Only three?" Boris repeated. "Are you sure?"

"Yeah, why?"

Boris pulled out his phone and scrolled before holding it out to show a text message. "Gene was watching their camp yesterday. Says early in the day, two snowmobiles set out heading west, carrying four guys."

No one said it; they didn't need to. Fear iced her veins as she realized Shayne might not be dead.

CHAPTER 13

*T*he fear in Rilee's eyes hit Mateo like a knife to the gut.

He'd failed her. Yes, he'd saved his bella from those kidnappers. Killed them so they could never come after her again, but he might have missed eliminating the man who gave her nightmares. The one who deserved to suffer most of all.

Not that she said anything about his failure. She didn't say much at all during the rest of that meeting even after it spilled from Reid's office to the larger meeting room. More residents joined them, male and female. Even a baby, cradled and asleep against Reid's shoulder.

There was much concern about the fact the remaining poachers at the hunting camp might retaliate. Even more worry that their secret might not be so secret anymore.

"We all knew this day was coming since Parker

opened his mouth and talked to the media," Reid announced loudly, quieting the arguing in the room. "With social media and everyone glued to their phones, it was only a matter of time. The important thing is how to deal with it."

"I say kill them all, dump their bodies in a lake, and pretend they were just some idiots thinking they could come to the great north and be dumb." Much like Gene, Boris had a one-track mind when it came to threats.

"And what of the next group?" Jan asked. "We can't kill everyone who knows what we are."

"Get rid of enough and they'll think twice before bothering us," Boris argued.

"This is my fault. They came looking for me." Rilee's shoulders slumped.

Reid snapped, "Don't you dare take the blame for this. If it's anyone's, it's mine. Obviously, we've got a leak somewhere." A traitor in their midst who put them all in danger.

On the ride back to the motel, Rilee hugged herself. More than once she had said she should probably sleep elsewhere.

His reply? "Like fuck. You belong with me." He planned to spend the evening reassuring her. With that in mind, he'd sent his mother a text saying they couldn't make it for dinner.

There was no reply.

Mamma only did that when mad. She'd have to wait. Rilee needed him.

He opened his hotel room door. A cleaning person

must have come by. The bed was crisply made. The carpet vacuumed. His shit...gone?

He couldn't see any of the packages his mother had sent. Or the clothes he'd draped on a chair. The drawers and closet were empty. His toiletries gone.

"Fuck me, did they think I checked out?" he growled.

"Um, Mateo. There's a note."

A note from his mother in Italian. Apparently, she'd anticipated he might make an excuse to be with Rilee.

He read it aloud in English. "I moved your things to the house I've been given during my stay. Come. I have lots of food."

"Guess you'd better go," she stated, her arms wrapped around her body, looking frail in his over-sized sweater.

"As if I'm leaving you alone," he said with a snort. "Besides she's expecting you."

"I highly doubt that."

He then proceeded to translate the shocking second half of the note. "Bring the girl."

She arched a brow. "Because that just screams welcome."

"More than you realize, bella. Shall we?"

The drive to the bungalow his mother managed to finagle took only a few minutes. The settlement tended to build dense, making travel between businesses and homes easy. The place sat square and single story. The chimney ran up the side, puffing smoke. The curtains were drawn, but light peeked around the edges. The red siding had faded from the sun and elements, and the front door didn't have anything to ring.

Rilee balked as he moved close enough to knock. She chewed her lower lip in obvious trepidation.

"Why do you look worried?"

"Because this is your mom."

"She is. Don't worry, I'm sure it will be fine."

She didn't appear convinced. "You are woefully naïve if you believe that. We slept together. Pretty sure that will make me public enemy number one."

"Probably." He wouldn't lie to her. He also reminded her, "You handled mamma fine earlier."

"Which I am now regretting," she muttered.

He grabbed her hands. She was wearing a pair of mittens he'd never worn but his mother insisted he pack. She also wore the matching hat and scarf and looked beautiful.

He wanted to say something reassuring; instead, he gave her a soft kiss.

"Was that supposed to help?"

"Should I try again?" he teased. "Because if you'd rather have more kisses, then we can go back to that hotel right now."

"What about your mother?"

"She can wait if you're not ready."

"She'd be so mad if you did that."

He shrugged. "This isn't about her, but you. What do you want?" Because that was what mattered.

Mamma would have to understand that Rilee had been through some stuff that made her leery of people. That required special handling.

"Refusing her invitation would set the wrong note." She wrinkled her nose. "I have to go in, even if it's just to be polite."

"It will be fine," he said, dropping another light kiss on her lips just as the door opened.

Light and heat spilled onto them, along with the aromatic delight of whatever was cooking on the stove.

Standing in the entrance, Mamma beamed. "There you are. How awful of that bear to keep everyone so late. Especially after your ordeal. You must be so hungry."

"Not as hungry as we would have been if you hadn't sent lunch. Delicious," he declared.

Mamma pretended as if it were nothing. A game they played, but a harmless one.

"You made all of it?" Rilee asked.

"Mamma is good at cooking for crowds." Then in an aside to his mother, "Rilee had two helpings of the potato salad."

She blushed as she stammered, "It was ridiculously good."

"I've made better, but I'm hindered by the lack of proper grocery shopping. Wait until I make you a really good one."

He almost drooled at the thought.

"I'm surprised you didn't volunteer to go with the

hunting party," Mamma said as she closed the door and pointed to the boot rack.

He knew better than to ask how she knew any of the meeting details. Mamma always knew more than she should. She'd probably grilled someone after she had them drop off that massive pile of sandwiches, the giant potato salad that Rilee had really enjoyed, and some kind of donut treat. It was devoured down to the last crumb. And he'd wager by now there wasn't a secret in town his mamma didn't know. He'd never been able to hide anything from her growing up.

"I didn't think I should leave Rilee alone."

"Smart thinking. And we will discuss it over dinner. I want to hear everything." The woman who couldn't be his mother with her genial smile clasped Rilee's hands. "Such an ordeal you've been through. No wonder you're so tiny, *piccini*. I made you some delicious things to put some meat on your bones."

"Smells amazing, Mamma," he declared, his stomach rumbling already as he stepped inside. He waited for his mother to welcome him. Depending on her mood, it could be a hug or a swat.

Mamma, though, was helping Rilee out of her coat.

"Thank you for the invitation, Mrs. Ricci," Rilee said stiffly, once more hugging her upper body.

"Bah, call me Mamma. It's what everyone does," she said with a bright smile.

Mateo stared. No one called her Mamma. That was his name for her.

"Are you feeling okay?" he asked.

His mother kept beaming. "Never better. Although I thought I raised you to be more useful. Don't just stand there, bambino. Hang up the coats." She thrust them at him and turned to Rilee. "Let's sit you by the stove where it's warm. Do you want a glass of milk with your dinner?" She took Rilee by the hand, tugging her down the narrow hall.

Rilee shot him a look of pure panic.

He really didn't know how to reply. This hadn't ever happened before. Was his mother trying some form of reverse psychology?

And where did this leave him, her favorite son? Apparently hanging up coats, and not sitting close to the fire or licking the spoon for the cake batter.

Dinner proved surreal, with his mother doing most of the talking. More surprising, after a while, Rilee was replying. Sometimes sarcastically, because that was her defense, but his mother seemed to expect it and even take enjoyment in the tiny barbs they darted back and forth. It was when they turned on him that the true danger in them teaming up became apparent.

"He's stubborn." Rilee agreed with something his mother said.

"He is, and so hard to potty train because of it. Why he was wetting his bed until he started school," his mother felt a need to say.

"She doesn't need to know that," he muttered.

"No, what she doesn't need to know is about the girly magazines you used to hide between your mattress and box spring. I thought he had more respect for women." His mother sniffed.

He forgave Mamma for spilling all his secrets because of Rilee's smile. "He's not a bad guy. He saved me. If it weren't for him, I'd have woken in a cage again."

"That is an awful thing to have happen," Mamma said. "I'm sorry.

Rilee shrugged. "I survived."

"And became strong. Such courage. It deserves cake."

Mamma had baked some concoction with icing and pudding.

Rilee moaned after each bite. "This is the most amazing thing I've ever eaten."

Which he found offensive. "Only because I never made you my upside-down peach cake."

Mamma sniffed. "Anyone can make that. This is the result of frothing the egg whites and perfectly blending the sugar and butter for the most consistent icing."

"Mine has brown sugar."

His mother pursed her lips. "Brown sugar is for pecan pie, peanut butter cookies, and caramel fudge."

"And here I thought it was only good for sprinkling on instant porridge," Rilee quipped.

Mateo shuddered. "That's not real porridge. Mamma, you have to make her some, with raisins."

"A grand plan for the morning. But now, I think little *piccini* needs to go to bed."

"I agree." He reached to grab Rilee's hand, only to have his mother beat him.

"Let's get you tucked in, *piccini*."

"I can handle it, Mamma," he grumbled.

Which was when his mother eyed him and said, "I don't think so. As my guest, Rilee gets the spare bedroom. You will sleep on the couch."

CHAPTER 14

*M*amma played chaperone, and Rilee almost laughed at the look on Mateo's face. But then again, hers must look as incredulous. She'd expected to spend dinner in battle with Mrs. Ricci—call me Mamma. More than a few times they had exchanged ripostes, only to laugh.

Laugh and eat good food. So much food. The woman didn't stop until Rilee leaned back and groaned. "I'm going to explode."

She certainly needed to sleep. All that food and warmth—and yes, a little wine—had her eyes drooping.

She didn't argue when mamma wanted to give her the double bed. What made her misty eyed? Laid on the comforter was a nightgown of soft flannel. The kind that went neck to ankle. It was obviously meant for her, given it was too short and narrow for the more voluptuous Mrs. Ricci.

"Thank you," she said, fingering the fabric. The

gesture was kind and more than she would have expected.

"I wasn't sure of your size other than too small. But I managed to find some things for you."

Some things? The tiny closet opened onto a dense forest of clothes. The bag on the dresser contained toiletries. And when she exited the bathroom, wearing her *Little House on the Prairie* getup, it was to find Mamma placing a book and a steaming mug of warm milk with a hint of cinnamon on top of the nightstand.

She couldn't help but blurt out, "Why are you being so nice to me?"

The reply was a simple, "I think it's overdue."

That was when the tears started. The arms enveloping her weren't corded with muscle, yet they offered the same kind of reassurance she got with Mateo. They showed caring.

But he didn't see it that way. He barged in barking, "What did you do to my bella?"

"Me?" His mother huffed. "While you were busy yapping and yapping all day long, you forgot to take care of this fragile creature. She is delicate, you giant meatball."

"I know she is!" he bellowed.

"Then you should take better care of her," his mother yelled back.

"I plan to!"

"Good." Mrs. Ricci left, and Rilee blinked at Mateo.

"Am I still high from the tranquilizers because I don't understand what's happening."

He opened his arms. "It's called family, bella."

"But she barely knows me."

"And? Some people you instantly feel a connection with the moment you meet. Like me and you."

She glanced at him but didn't know what to reply. Because meeting him had changed something in her. In how she felt. In what she wanted.

He cupped her face and dropped a kiss on her lips. "You aren't alone anymore."

Not yet, but she couldn't be sure of tomorrow or the next day, which was why she threw her arms around his neck and deepened the chaste kiss. She plastered herself to him, wanting what only he could give her. Needing the pleasure.

They were quiet, so very, very quiet, but that didn't stop the hollered, "Not before you're married!"

He sighed as he pulled away. "We should have stayed at the motel."

Whereas she grinned and felt bold enough to say, "Wait until she falls asleep."

"Bella," he breathed as he gave her one final kiss and left.

She lay in her bed. Wide-awake. Anticipating.

The door remained partially ajar, meaning she could hear him and his mother bickering about nothing but with a warmth and affection that actually lulled her to sleep. A nap as it turned out because the moment her door creeped open she woke.

"Bella?" he whispered.

Rather than reply, she reached for him. He slid into

the bed with her, wearing only his track pants and nothing else. Hungry lips met and slid with passionate abandon. Tongues twined, and as they kissed, her gown rode up, baring her to his roaming touch.

Her feverish skin pressed against his, her erect nipples rubbing his chest. He stopped kissing her only that he might tug those buds with his lips, pulling and sucking, while she shoved a fist in her mouth so she wouldn't make any noise.

She wanted to yell her pleasure. Wanted to scream and beg him to stop teasing. All she could do was writhe then buck as his fingers slid past her panties and against her wet slit. He used her own honey to rub against her clit. The friction had her trembling with need.

She finally gasped, "Please." She needed him inside her. Now.

But he seemed intent on teasing. She shoved at him when he softly said, "Is something wrong?"

"Yeah, you're taking too long," was her complaint. She forced him onto his back and tugged at his pants. He lifted his hips to help her ease them down.

Then, because it seemed only fair, she grabbed hold of him and stroked. Stroked until he was the one writhing and breathing hard, finally growling, "Bella."

Only then did she straddle him, hovering her sex over the head of his cock, teasing him. She wanted to tease him some more and inserted just the tip of his shaft. The problem being it wasn't only torture for him.

She dropped herself onto him, impaling herself

with his whole length with a gasp that saw her head going back, her nails digging into his chest, and his fingers clutching at her hips. For a moment they were still, his cock throbbing inside. Slowly, so very slowly, she started to move, rocking back and forth, grinding herself hard enough that her clit got some pressure. Angling so he hit her sweet spot inside.

It was hard to maintain a rhythm, distracted as she was by the pleasure. He helped, his hands clasping her hips, pulling and pushing her to give her the friction she needed. Building her pleasure.

Just before she came, she folded that their lips might meet, and he muffled the cry she almost let loose. He held her as she shook and quivered, the climax almost too much to bear.

She collapsed on him, and he held her close.

They fell asleep, intertwined, until dawn when the sound of a door shutting woke them.

"Shit. Mamma's up." He gave her a quick kiss before sliding out of bed. He tossed her a wink at the door as he slipped out.

She grinned like an idiot.

Then blushed like a tomato when, at breakfast, Mamma asked, "How was your night?"

And he declared, "Very satisfying."

CHAPTER 15

*I*t was when Rilee was showering that his mamma cornered Mateo and wagged a finger. "Don't think I don't know what happened last night."

"Whatever do you mean?" he replied, playing innocent.

"That girl deserves better than you toying with her heart."

"That girl is going to be my wife."

Words that should have sent his mamma into a rant, but instead, she smiled. "Good. I like her."

He frowned. "Is this some sort of reverse psychology where you liking her is supposed to make me dump her?"

"No. It's me giving my approval. She'll make you a fine mate. She's strong and won't put up with your nonsense."

"She also won't tolerate yours."

"Exactly," was his mother's reply.

Given he couldn't be sure the danger to Rilee was gone, he wouldn't leave the house until his mother insisted. "Go. Visit with the men and plan stupid things. The girl and I will be fine without you. We're going to make dumplings."

"We are?" Rilee asked entering for the last part of their conversation, skin dewy and wet hair slicked back.

"And I will show you how to knit," Mamma declared.

He expected Rilee to beg him for rescue, but instead, she nodded. "That would be useful. Thanks."

What was happening in his world? This wasn't how it was supposed to unfold!

Sauntering over to Reid's office, he arrived in time for Gene's text. *Subjects on the move.*

Not toward town, but away from it. Apparently, they'd noticed the missing hunters and assumed them lost in the storm and cut the hunting trip short. Search crews were being assembled, many of them volunteers from Kodiak Point to avoid suspicion, and to cover any traces Mateo might have missed.

The news of their departure should have eased Mateo's fear, but the problem was Gene couldn't confirm Rilee's abductor was in the group. They wore helmets concealing their faces, and even if they hadn't, Rilee couldn't give them more than a basic description of the asshole, Shayne.

"How do we not have a picture?" Mateo growled.

Boris was the one to mutter, "Because the name he gave her was fake. There is no Shayne Klondike. At least not one that she recognized. And believe me we tried searching every database we could."

"What of the poachers? Did we get a list of identities? I've got people I can call who can dig up dirt on them."

"No names. And the pictures we've managed haven't been great. It's as if they knew they were being watched and never left their shelters with their faces uncovered."

He spent the afternoon waiting for more news, but it wasn't until that evening that their contact in the next town confirmed the surviving hunters had arrived and despite their desire to leave, were having to answer questions about the missing people in their party. Good for Kodiak Point? Not really, because it seemed too easy.

Which was why he spent that evening on the phone, making arrangements. The next morning, he sprang the news.

"We're leaving Kodiak Point."

Rilee, sitting by his mother on the couch, knitting needles in hand, trying to keep up, stopped for a moment and said, "Oh." Just one small sound.

"It's best we go. I've made arrangements to take us into the next town this morning. And then a flight back home."

"I hope you have a safe trip." Judging by Rilee's crestfallen features, she'd totally misunderstood.

"*We* are leaving. As in you, me, and Mamma."

That brought a frown. "Me?"

"Yes you. It's not safe here."

"Why?" Only to turn pale. "So he is alive."

"I don't know. The hunters left, but we couldn't confirm he was one of them. And even if he was..." He didn't finish the thought because she understood. With the enemy aware of where she lived, could she ever be safe?

He expected her to argue about leaving with him. Had prepared a few replies.

To his surprise, she instead asked, "Where are we going?

It was Mamma who said, "We're going home."

Boris drove them into town in an SUV equipped with chains and extra gas cans strapped to the roof. They made it and onto a plane, all without mishap—if one ignored Rilee's blanched features and her tears as she hugged people goodbye.

On the plane, she sat between him and his mother. They each held one of her hands for takeoff. Then his mother kept her occupied with knitting, the clack of the needles a soothing sound that put him to sleep. He needed to be rested for the next leg of their trip.

The car was in the parking lot, as arranged, keys in the wheel well.

Rilee watched him adjust the driver seat and mirrors before asking, "Whose car is this?"

"Not mine." At her rounded mouth, he added, "A

friend is loaning it to me in order to keep us off the grid. We're going for a long drive, so buckle up."

He drove across three states, stopping too many times so that his mother could stretch her legs but also so that Rilee could get some air. She didn't say much. She didn't have to. He could read the nervousness in her. It killed him. If he'd only done a better job that day. Known there was a fourth assailant he'd missed. It hurt him to know he'd failed her.

How could he fix this? He hoped bringing her home would help. She certainly seemed intrigued.

"You live in suburbia?" she'd stated looking around at the houses all built in the seventies during the housing boom, which erupted when manufacturing powered the middle class.

"It's a great neighborhood."

"I'm sure it is." She eyed the split-level brick home, with its black shingle roof and bay window, with a small smile. Her gaze hit the detached garage, installed by his father with a loft over it—to give him some manspace, as he called it.

Mamma said, "That's where Mateo sleeps. You will be in the house with me."

And no amount of arguing on his part would change her damned mind because it wasn't proper, don't you know.

He'd tried hissing, "She's my mate."

His mamma's pert reply, "No ring. No mark. No go."

A ring, he could buy. The mark? Would Rilee agree?

Sure, the last few days had been amazing. She'd welcomed him to her bed with eagerness. Smiled when she saw him. Beat him at cards and wasn't afraid to bask in her win.

However, when she thought no one was looking, her face pinched, her expression turned worried. She chewed her lip, but worst of all were the nightmares each night. Each time she woke whimpering, he soothed her, because, despite his mother's decree, he still spent each night with her, fleeing before dawn. Not fooling anyone.

He installed cameras and security on the windows and doors. He spent most of his time inside with Rilee and his mom, working on a laptop at the dining room table. When he got phone calls that he worried might upset Rilee, he took them outside.

However, despite having her in his childhood home, flourishing under his mother's eye, being kept safe under his watchful stare, he knew she was afraid.

Which might have led to him being a tad overprotective. It was his mother that finally got him to leave her side when Rilee complained she just wanted to be able to go to the bathroom without him checking on her. She didn't understand the panic that filled him when she was out of sight.

Mamma did. "The scariest thing in life is not always being by the side of the one you love."

"How do I stop feeling like that?" he asked. "After what happened to her, I just don't want her to ever be hurt again."

"You can't guarantee it even if you're with her every second of every day. What I can guarantee is if you don't give her space, she'll probably kill you."

"But you'd avenge me, right?" he asked.

"Maybe. Depends."

"Seriously?"

"Well, she would be justified. You are being an annoying meatball."

Which led to a round of bickering that Rilee joined, and turned into a dinner of handmade gnocchi, fresh Alfredo sauce, and garlic-butter sautéed vegetables.

They enjoyed a tenuous happiness that could be easily broken. He had to do something. Had to fix this, he just didn't know how.

Then he got the call...

"We think we've found the target."

CHAPTER 16

*T*he door to her cabin opened, and there were those eyes, the same ones that taunted her for years. The mask did nothing to disguise him.

This time, she didn't freeze but dove for her gun leaning beside the door. Before she could wrap her fingers around it, a hard shove sent her tumbling. Suddenly the cottage was gone, and she was in that basement again, the room with two doors made of solid metal, both locked when she was inside.

A gallery, higher than she could leap, ringed the room, the railing made of glass, tall enough that no spectator could accidentally fall.

No escape.

She padded around on four feet, pacing the concrete floor with the smell of blood that a scrub and rinse couldn't erase. The drain in the middle an efficiency that was also a necessity. The violence usually turned messy.

Today her opponent wasn't an animal, or a shifter like her. It was him, wearing black leather and steel-toed boots.

He had that whip with the silver barbs, flashy and painful. Worse than that, in his other hand he held the cattle prod. Used enough times, it made a person piss themselves.

No. Not again. She growled and paced.

"Now, now, Rilee Smiley." His stupid nickname for her. "Is that any way to say hello to your master?" His voice held a nasal twang.

She hissed.

"We can do this the easy way, or the hard." He cracked the whip. "What's it going to be? You going to show this crowd how special you are, or how tough?"

The answer never changed no matter the pain. She charged.

Zap. A lightning bolt of pure pain shot through her. She arched and screamed and—

Startled awake. Rilee huffed hotly, panic making her thrash against the arms holding her. It took his insistent, "Bella, wake up. It's me. You're safe," before she could calm enough to control her breathing.

Mateo's closeness comforted, and for a moment, she leaned into his strength. How many times would she wake him a terrified, sour mess before he had enough?

It seemed trite to mumble, "I'm sorry."

"Don't you dare apologize," he growled. "This is my fault. I should have never left you that day. I should have…"

Would have. Could have. Should have. The guilt they both suffered would have made her laugh if it weren't so sad.

Here she was with a guy who might be cocky but showered her with kindness. It was shocking to realize, even with her fear revived, she'd never been happier. And it wasn't just because of Mateo.

She'd worried about living with Mamma, was convinced at some point the nice lady who'd taken her under her tiger's paw would turn into a hellcat who showed her true feelings about Rilee.

Only Mamma got even nicer. She took care of Rilee in a way she'd never imagined but seen in movies, like a real mom would.

But could she relax and enjoy it? Not completely. She'd never been more anxious. The other shoe would drop. Probably on her head.

Life couldn't really be this good. This happy. It wouldn't last.

The end happened during breakfast. Mateo received a text, and his face went through so many expressions, but it was his quick glance at her that made her blurt out, "What happened?"

"Nothing."

She glared. "Is that your final answer? Your way of acting as if I'm not capable of handling adult subject matter?"

A cuff behind his ear rocked his head as Mamma huffed, "I didn't raise you to be a sexist pig."

"I'm not being an ass. The news isn't that big of a deal."

Rilee arched a brow. "Then why not tell me?"

"They might have a lead on the guy you know as Shayne."

She felt the color leaving her face.

He sighed. "And this is why I didn't want to tell you."

"He's my problem, not yours."

"Oh, he's my problem all right," he growled. "And if I could leave, I'd show him what I thought of guys who beat on girls."

She narrowed her gaze on him. "Why can't you leave? And be very careful about your reply."

"I'm not going to pretend that I'm not concerned about you. I abandoned you once, and you were attacked. I won't leave you vulnerable again."

"Instead, you'd leave that sick man to roam. Great plan," was her sarcastic reply.

"What do you expect me to do?" he exploded.

"I expect you to do your job. Aren't you some kind of enforcer for the council?" Rilee declared.

"Yes, but—"

"No buts. Your job is to keep our kind safe, and we both know so long as Shayne lives, he poses a danger."

"I agree, but you also can't just expect me to leave you."

"If you have a lead on Shayne, then that means he's not here. Right?" Rilee questioned.

"The guy they're watching is in New York but—"

"But what?"

"What if it's not him?"

"Easy enough to figure out. Show me a picture."

When he didn't reply, she sighed. "You don't even have a picture?"

"None of the images on file are any good."

"What about his driver's license?" asked his mother.

"None because it was obtained in a state that allows people to refuse based on their religious beliefs. It doesn't help he's some VIP's kid and has been shielded from the media."

"Rich enough and apparently powerful enough he's probably untouchable," she murmured. "Meaning he'll never go away."

He surged from his seat, only to get on his knees in front of her. "Don't say that. I won't let him hurt you."

"You can't promise that." No one could.

"You need to do a stakeout," his mother declared.

"Don't you start with me, Mamma. I'm still getting flak for the last one when you kept calling to ask if I needed coffee and donuts." He glared at his mother, who continued to knit without missing a beat.

"Excuse me for making sure you're not hungry," his mother huffed indignantly.

"Stakeouts should be discreet, not have you showing up in curlers with a brown paper bag and a thermos."

The cuteness of it didn't help her anxiety. It went rocketing, leaving her vibrating and uneasy. "I need to…" She stood and moved away from him toward the door, only to realize she didn't know where to go.

Before she could open it, he'd slid into her path. "You're not leaving."

"Staying here puts you in danger."

He snorted. "Don't play martyr with me, bella. You're safer here than out there."

"I know. But I'm scared." Her shoulders slumped at the hated admission.

A finger tipped her chin. His grave gaze met hers. "I'm going to take care of this, bella. Now. Today."

"I thought you couldn't leave."

"I won't have you living in fear. I can't."

He kissed her, and it went on until Mamma yelled from the kitchen, "I packed you a lunch for the trip."

Rilee sat quietly on the bed as he stuffed a bag. She welcomed their quick coupling where the clothes were just shifted aside and quickly righted before a certain someone walked in on them. She held back tears as he gave her a long kiss goodbye.

He'd be fine. This was the kind of thing he did all the time. Still, she leaned into Mamma's embrace and took solace in her whispered, "My boy will fix this. You'll see. Come, let's go make some fettuccine for dinner."

Mateo kept in touch, calling her that night once he landed. The next day, he texted first thing. Called her again. It was midafternoon and his third call of the day when she rolled her eyes as she answered with a laugh. "You again?"

"Hey, bella. Do you miss me?"

More than he could imagine. "Not really. Your mom made me some kind of tomato soup for lunch that was to die for."

"If you're trying to make me jealous, it's working," he grumbled.

She laughed again. "Maybe I miss you a little."

"I miss you a whole lot," he admitted. "But that's not the reason I called. I have a picture finally."

She didn't need to ask of whom. "Can you text it?" she asked in a raspy voice.

The moment she saw it, she felt her knees go weak and she leaned against a wall.

"Bella?" Urgency lit his tone.

It took her two breaths before she could say, "I'm here. It's him."

He didn't ask if she was sure. "I'll take care of this, bella. Trust me."

She did. But that didn't fix the dread. The nightmares were especially harsh that night.

Meaning she was tired the next morning and grumpier than usual, especially since Mateo didn't call. She missed him and really wished she hadn't forced him to leave. She could have used his arms hugging her.

Calls to his phone went right to voicemail. Had he turned it off? Was he okay?

Mamma didn't seem too worried, which was the only reason Rilee didn't panic.

The doorbell rang, and Mamma shouted, "I'm watching the soup. Can you get that?"

Given Mrs. Ricci's love affair with online shopping, deliveries tended to happen daily, sometimes more than once a day. Still, Rilee showed caution before answering and peeked outside. A delivery truck was parked across the end of driveway and a guy in tan slacks and shirt stood on the step, holding a package. She opened the door, and the delivery person turned, lips upturned, sharp blue eyes practically dancing with mirth.

"If it isn't my missing lynx."

Given a part of her had been waiting for this to happen, she reacted quickly, the door barely open before she slammed it shut and yelled, "Danger! Call Mateo."

For once Mrs. Ricci didn't ask questions, which was odd. Rilee whirled to glance down the hall, unable to see past the wall into the kitchen.

At her back, Shayne wasn't happy she'd shut the door on him. "You can't escape, Rilee. I own you. I bought you."

Bought her from a mother more interested in her next fix. The first time selling her secret, which led to Shayne seducing her. Then a second betrayal giving her location, leading to her capture.

"Go to hell."

"Open this fucking door!" He pounded on it.

She retreated, wishing she had her rifle. It might have penetrated the door. Shayne wouldn't be so annoying with a bullet in his chest.

She didn't pivot until she'd reached the mid-point in the hall, and then she took quick, quiet steps into the kitchen. It was odd Mamma wasn't saying a damned word. The woman constantly talked, even if she didn't expect a reply. She chattered as she cooked. Knitted. Cleaned. The only time she ever stayed quiet for any length of time was when watching *The Witcher*. Apparently Geralt was her type of man, which made Mateo groan and whine about her being his mother. To wit, Rilee added something about his mom being in her sexual prime. He blanched and went to go find something manly to do, leaving her giggling with Mrs. Ricci.

Mamma would be fine. She had to be.

Except she wasn't.

Rilee walked into the kitchen to see Mamma sprawled on the floor.

"No," she huffed, ready to rush to her side, only a whisper of movement warned her.

She ducked, and the tranquilizing dart only just missed her. A strange woman with dark hair scraped in a severe ponytail stood and took aim again, forcing Rilee to take cover behind the island, in sight of Mrs. Ricci.

Her eyes were closed, her face slack, but Rilee could see her chest moving, so still alive. It didn't help much. The thing she feared most had come to pass. She'd brought harm upon those who tried to care of her.

She duck-walked around the island as the woman took steps to try and get a clean shot. Rilee hadn't even noticed the pounding at the front door had ceased until Shayne stepped into the kitchen and she was suddenly penned between a tranquilizer and a sadistic place.

A triumphant smile tugged Shayne's lips. "Nice to

see you, again. In the flesh. What do you say we keep you that way for a while?"

The icy fear coursing through her veins had her panting. She knew what he meant. Why he wanted her in this shape.

"I'd rather die," she replied, standing and grabbing for the handle of a knife.

"Don't be so dramatic. Behave and maybe I'll even let you hold the creatures when they're born." He took a step forward.

"I'll never go in a cage again."

She whirled and threw the knife, hitting the woman in the arm. She dropped the gun. Before Rilee could whirl back, Shayne was on her, grabbing for her hair in his fist, even as he tasered her with his other hand.

Her knees turned to rubber, and her teeth clacked as the electricity jolted through her. The pain in her scalp as he held her off the floor by the hair barely registered.

She hung limp in his grasp, eyes downcast, pretending to be submissive. When he would have yanked her upright, she punched, nailing him in the nutsack.

He yelled and let go. She hit the floor hard on her knees and bounced up, grabbing another knife, only to have the woman attack. They grappled, the larger female having a weight advantage that saw them slamming into the counters, topping dishes. But Rilee managed to grab another knife and slash the woman's arm. The blood dripping from her attacker rendered the floor slick. They slipped and fell. The knife she held got stuck.

In a body.

Rilee pushed off the gasping woman as she clutched the knife embedded in her stomach.

"I am really wondering if you're worth the trouble," Shayne declared.

Rilee turned to see the gun aimed at her head.

"She is, but you're not." From behind, Mamma—looking grim and vicious—grabbed Shayne around the neck and dropped to the floor. The loud crack was the kind no one would ever get up and walk away from.

Shayne's limp body didn't move. He was dead.

Rilee burst into tears.

Comforting arms wrapped around her. "There, there, *piccini*, it's all right. Mamma took care of the bad man. No more nightmares for you."

"You could have died," she sobbed.

"Please. We knew they'd be more interested in kidnapping than killing."

The words penetrated, and she pulled out of the embrace. "Wait a second. What's this we thing? You expected this to happen?" she asked, gaping at Mamma.

"It's why we sent Mateo away." Mrs. Ricci held the most serious mien for a moment. She patted her hair. "We knew this miscreant wouldn't come after you while Mateo was around. My boy might be a giant meatball, but he's also dangerous."

"But not dangerous enough to deter you from this crazy plan!" Mateo suddenly bellowed.

CHAPTER 17

*T*he smile that lit Rilee's face when she whirled to face him hit Mateo hard.

When he'd realized the man he'd been watching had slipped through their net, he'd panicked. It didn't help he couldn't call and worry Rilee, so he called his mother instead. She'd been entirely too calm and collected.

And she'd been lying.

But he'd confront her about that in a moment. Rilee squealed his name, "Mateo!" before she flew into his arms.

He lifted her off the floor in a hug that he had to restrain lest it crack a few ribs. He buried his face in her hair. Held her for a moment, until the anger and tension in him demanded a reply. Setting her down, her kept his arm around her and glared at his mother. "What did you do, Mamma? Did you plan for Rilee to be attacked by that piece of shit?" He scowled at the body on the floor.

At least his mother had killed the asshole clean. No blood, unlike the other cooling body. That would take some scrubbing to erase.

"It wasn't just me planning this. Terrence was involved."

His boss? He began to shake with anger. "He sent me out of town on purpose?"

"Because he knew you'd never agree to using Rilee as bait."

"No fucking shit I would have said no. I would never put Rilee in danger." He raked fingers through his hair. "What I don't understand is how they got past Terrence's guards. He was supposed to have a rotating pair watching the house at all times."

"And they're still watching. Who do you think advised me that a delivery truck had passed by three times since yesterday? Same plates. No stops to deliver anything."

"And you didn't call me?" he said in a low growl. Rilee put her hand on him, soothing the beast, but only barely.

"I didn't want you to worry in case it was nothing." Mamma lifted her chin.

"Do you call this nothing?" He pointed to the bodies on the floor.

Rilee stepped out of his hug to confront him, standing between him and his mother. "Your mother saved my life."

"She put you in danger." He seethed with the knowledge of it.

"Only to help her," Mamma said. "When I found out the target slipped surveillance, I had a hunch he was coming here."

"How did you even know? That's classified intel."

Mamma folded her hands. "I know. Who do you think has told everyone to keep a lid on this mess?" Her serious mien had him gaping.

"*You!* You work for the council?" He might have squeaked. "How did I not know?"

"Because I'm just that good," was Mamma's smug reply. "I can't believe you never figured it out."

"You can't be a council member. You're Mamma. You bake. And drive me nuts. You knit and do crafts. Not run the world."

"I'm a multitasker."

"But how? You were always home when I was growing up."

His mother snorted. "Get with the times, bambino. Most work is done via the phone, or through a secure network."

He thought of all the times he'd come into the kitchen to see her nose pressed to the laptop screen, baking ingredients spread all around her. A sham...

"All this time..." He shook his head.

"You never saw because you never wanted to. Did you ever stop and wonder why I insisted you learn how to fight?"

"I assume it was because you were terrible at it."

She'd only taken him to the range a few times, where her ineptness proved embarrassing to a competitive boy.

"I failed on purpose because I didn't want you to know."

"Why not?"

"A woman likes secrets." Mamma shrugged. "Given you didn't know, I figured *he* wouldn't either. He assumed us defenseless." She tossed a look at the dead man.

"But how did you shake off the sedative?" Riley asked.

"Easy. I wore a vest under my sweaters." Mamma patted her stomach.

"Protecting your chest and nothing else," he remarked.

His mother snorted. "Even if they got me in the arm or leg, one puny tranquilizer wouldn't have taken me out. The plan all along was to pretend it worked to ease anyone attacking into a false sense of security. When the time was right, I acted."

"Why did you wait so long?" Rilee asked.

"You needed a chance to fight back. To see your enemy taken out. With the threat gone, and you having a hand in it, maybe you'll stop having nightmares."

"Putting her in danger was not the solution," he boomed.

Mamma snorted. "She was never in danger. The miscreant didn't want to kill her."

"Just put her in a cage to torture her some more," he

spat, only to apologize to Rilee. "Sorry, bella. I don't mean to be a crude."

"It's okay. I'm fine. Everything worked out." She tried to soothe him, but he was still angry.

"You overstepped, Mamma. You had no right."

"I have every right to protect my daughter." Mamma lifted her chin.

"What daughter?" Rilee asked stupidly. "I thought Mateo was an only child."

"You, of course," exclaimed Mamma.

"Now who's the meathead," he muttered.

Rilee blinked. "You think of me as a daughter? But you barely know me."

"As if that matters." At her expression, Mamma grabbed her into a hug. "I didn't know what a perfectly angelic boy Mateo would turn out to be when he was born, and yet I loved him anyways. You already have an advantage over him because you come potty trained. Plus, I always wanted a daughter."

"And you want me?" She sounded so surprised.

"Yes, you. I think you make a fine daughter. If a bit skinny. We need to feed you more."

"I've been eating three meals and two snacks a day already," Rilee muttered with a small smile.

"Now that this ordeal is over, I think we should bake something."

"And by we, she means just herself," Mateo noted.

His mother didn't look the slightest bit abashed. "You like pie? I haven't made one since you got here. Tell me your favorite flavor."

Rilee's shoulders rolled. "I don't think I have one. I didn't get much pie growing up. Just a few store-bought versions."

Horror twisted his mother's lips. "No. Oh no. We must fix this. At once." Mamma moved for the pantry.

"Council member my ass," he grumbled. "Hello, have you forgotten the bodies in the kitchen?"

His mother eyed them. "Good thing the freezer has room. Fetch the meat grinder from the basement."

At dual-exclaimed, "Mamma!" she gave them a toothy grin. "Just kidding. I've already signaled for a cleanup crew."

The crew consisted of a four-person team plus Terrence, who got a tongue-lashing from Mateo.

"I can't believe you actually agreed to use Rilee as bait."

"You're only pissed because you found the missing lynx in your life." No need to ask how Terrence knew. It was obvious to him, and apparently everyone else.

As he'd stated what seemed like too long ago, Riley was his mate. And it was past time he did something about it.

"Yeah. She's the one." But he was totally going to punch his boss in the face if he gloated about it.

The bodies were removed, all trace evidence scrubbed. Mamma kicked them out of the kitchen to cook up a feast while he snuggled Rilee in his lap, napping while she read a book. One of the nicest, most relaxing things he'd ever done.

Dinner was a delicious chicken paprika with

biscuits to dip in the gravy. Dessert was four different pies, the ones Mamma figured Rilee would like most.

As Rilee declared cherry her absolute favorite, he knew it was time.

He slid from his chair onto a knee beside her. Produced the ring from his pocket—given to him by Mamma the day after they arrived from Kodiak Point. The ring his father had given her.

"Just in case," she'd said with a smile.

As if there was any doubt this would happen.

He held out the ring, and it caught Rilee's gaze. "Bella, we met only recently, but I knew then, and am even more certain now, that you are the one. I love you. Say you'll be my wife. My mate. My partner for life."

His mother sobbed.

Rilee gaped at him, her eyes flooding with tears.

Oh shit. She was gonna say no.

He'd asked too soon.

Fuck me—

She was in his arms, muttering yes over and over while kissing him. He liked the kissing part, so wouldn't you know his mother interrupted and insisted they have champagne.

Funny thing, it was already chilling in an ice bucket.

And then, with that ring on Rilee's finger, they went to bed together, holding hands and taking the stairs to his loft over the garage two at a time.

The moment the door closed, she was in his arms. Kissing him. Touching him.

And he was right there touching her back.

They made love quickly that first time, a rough, hard pounding that had her clawing his back and yelling for more.

Then more softly, tenderly. Afterward he held her dewy body and thanked the moon goddess she'd come through her ordeal safe.

For the first time since they'd first slept together, she had no nightmares, and she woke in the morning with a smile.

But that was all he got since Mamma had no boundaries!

EPILOGUE

*S*pending a night in the loft didn't stop Mamma from barging in. The next morning, they woke to the smell of coffee and pastries. Rilee's mouth watered as she sat up, thankfully wearing Mateo's shirt.

Mateo, wearing nothing at all under the covers, scowled. "Mamma, a little privacy, please."

"Bah. As if I haven't seen it all before. Who do you think washed that tushy when you were little?"

"Mamma," he growled.

Rilee giggled and kept laughing that day, and the next…

They got married in front of Reid and the gang in Kodiak Point, and after, they honeymooned on a Norwegian cruise. When that was over, they chose to live with Mamma—who almost burst into tears the one time Rilee slipped and called her Mrs. Ricci. She'd had to listen to the lament of how hurt Mamma was, because didn't Rilee know she loved her?

She knew. It was stifling. And amazing.

The woman, who kept true to her claim to treat Rilee as a daughter, had plans drawn up to remodel the master bedroom of the house into something modern with an ensuite bathroom that included a soaker tub. Rilee couldn't wait to sink into it.

Mamma would take over the loft, but the kitchen in the house would remain her domain. Rilee was more than happy to be the one sitting and licking a spoon as she begged for a taste.

"What's this?" Mateo asked, pointing at the blue-prints to a cheater door leading to the room next to the master.

"Your mom had them install it for easy access to the nursery," Rilee said, sliding her arms around him and peeking around his body at the plans laid out on the table.

"She's not very subtle," he remarked somewhat ruefully.

"No, but she is pretty awesome, and it's nice to know that, unlike my childhood, our kids won't struggle because they'll have an epic grandmother."

"You say that now, but you just wait until you get pregnant," he declared. "She will drive you insane."

"You think she'll be a little overprotective?" she teased.

"She'll have rolls of bubble wrap delivered before you're done announcing it."

"And you'll be what? Mr. Calm, Cool, and Collected?"

"Totally," he boasted.

"Glad to hear it because I've got a wager with your mom that you won't freak out when you find out we're pregnant with twins."

Thump.

He hit the floor, and she sighed, especially since Mamma stalked in, holding out her hand. "Told you the meatball couldn't handle it. Pay up."

"Fine. You win. We can get our nails done this afternoon." Something she'd balked at as being too girly.

Mamma beamed as if she'd won a prize.

Rilee never planned to let her know she'd lost that wager on purpose.

She knew Mateo would go overboard. He had the house baby-proofed before her first trimester was even done. His mamma was the one to be the voice of reason when he got to be a little bit too much, carrying her up and down every flight of stairs, even the single step into the sunken living room.

He was overprotective, but amazing. And she finally understood what family meant. It was all about the love. A love that would last forever.

BUT THIS ISN'T THE END... GET READY TO HIT THE SKIES WITH A BROKEN soldier in Iron Eagle.

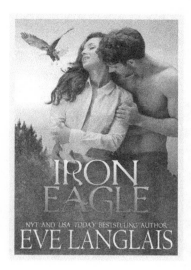

AFTERWORD

Wow, was it ever nice to come back to Kodiak Point and see a few familiar faces. You know what that means? Keep an eye open because, now that I've had a taste, I'm hungry to write more.

In case you didn't know, Kodiak Point was the starting place for two other series. Bitten Point, which links right off the end of Grizzly Love, and then Dragon Point. So if you like action, drama, romance, and snarky interactions, be sure to grab the entire series.

~Happy reading, Eve